# Just a Cowboy's Fairy Tale

## Flyboys of Sweet Briar Ranch in North Dakota
### Book Nine
### Jessie Gussman

Published By: Jessie Gussman

# Contents

# Acknowledgments

**Cover art by Julia Gussman**
**Editing by Heather Hayden**
**Narration by Jay Dyess**
**Author Services by CE Author Assistant**

Listen to a FREE professionally performed and produced audiobook version of this title on Youtube. Search for "Say With Jay" to browse all available FREE Dyess/Gussman audiobooks.

# Chapter 1

"Look at the camera and smile."

Eliza Walton took her own advice, looking at Melinda Watts, who held her phone up, snapping pictures of her beloved son, Randy, who sat on Billy, the famous matchmaking steer of Sweet Water, North Dakota.

Billy was moonlighting on his second job today. That of petting zoo star.

Somehow, Eliza had gotten nominated to be in charge of Billy for the end-of-summer Harvest Festival.

"You did great, honey," Melinda said as she came over, her arms outstretched to Randy.

"I want to stay on," Randy said, sticking his lower lip out.

"But there's a whole line of children. We have to let everyone have a turn," Melinda said, very reasonably.

Eliza could see that Randy wasn't the slightest bit interested in the logical argument his mother used.

"Everyone who gets a picture with Billy also gets a lollipop. Kenni is handing them out right over there," Eliza said, pointing to her good friend Kennedy, who had recently married Baker Lawrence.

Funny that she and Kenni would end up being such good friends, considering that she was a reporter—ex-reporter—and Kenni had spent the last decade running from the paparazzi.

That was probably part of the reason why Eliza had quit her job. She had never been part of a pack of paparazzi, chasing famous people, trying to get that one pic that would make her rich. But she had made a living writing stories about people who hadn't necessarily wanted stories written about them.

She had been dissatisfied in her job for a long time, but her friendship with Kenni had solidified her decision to leave Houston and move to Sweet Water.

Crazy decision, according to all of her city friends, since she had no job lined up.

Unless one counted what she was currently doing, being the keeper of the petting zoo, but it didn't pay.

She grinned engagingly at Randy, grateful that she and Kenni had discussed the fact that many children wouldn't want to leave the steer and that they would need something to entice them. The lollipops had been a great idea.

Randy looked over at Kenni, who held a lollipop up, her exposed teeth blue. After giving the steer a last hug, Randy hopped down and ran over, demanding a blue lollipop. His hapless mother followed, after shooting an apologetic yet grateful smile at Eliza.

"You're a popular boy," Eliza said, petting Billy's neck.

The steer stood contentedly chewing his cud, seeming oblivious to all the noise going on around him. He was a natural for the petting zoo.

Eliza had heard all the stories about him being a matchmaking steer, but she felt that was just something small-town people had a tendency to exaggerate.

Being from the city, she was a lot more jaded and certainly a lot more skeptical about stories that had no basis in actual fact.

A matchmaking steer? Cute.

"Who's next?" she asked, turning back to the line of children.

A sweet little girl timidly raised her hand.

"I think Billy loves ponytails," she said as she walked to the little girl, looking at her mom before kneeling down. She had already had several children who wanted to ride but were scared, and chatting with them a bit first helped ease their fears.

The girl grinned broadly and touched her hair. "Like mine?"

"Just like that. And you have two, which should make Billy extra happy."

"Mommy did it," the little girl said, tugging on her mother's hand.

"And she did an excellent job," Eliza said, gently touching the shiny curls that looped out of the tight ponytails.

"Does Billy really like ponytails?"

"He seems to. I think he likes little girls better than little boys too." She lifted her eyes and looked down the line at the assortment of boys and girls still waiting. "But don't tell anyone," she said, her voice lowered to a conspiratorial whisper, drawing the little girl in to her by sharing a secret.

The little girl shrugged her shoulders and ducked her head, giggling a little.

"My name's Eliza," Eliza said, holding out her hand.

The little girl looked at it. "I'm Chloe," she said, still not sure what to do with Eliza's hand.

"You're supposed to shake her hand, Chloe," her mother said, her hands on her shoulders as she leaned down over her daughter.

"Oh," Chloe said, carefully reaching out and taking Eliza's hand.

Eliza gave her a squeeze and a little shake before she said, "Are you ready to pet Billy?"

"I want to ride him. But I want to see you do it first."

"Me?" Eliza said, feeling a strange twist in her stomach. So far, she'd gotten quite used to petting Billy. All he did was stand there and chew, occasionally grabbing another bite of hay from the large pile in front of him. But as for actually getting on his back, she hadn't done it, hadn't planned on it, and, if she were being honest, definitely didn't want to.

"She always feels better if she sees someone else do it first. Someone she trusts," the mom said over Chloe's head, her hands still on both shoulders.

It was on the tip of Eliza's tongue to suggest that the mom get on Billy, but she supposed that as the zookeeper, she was probably the one who ought to set the example.

She wasn't exactly an expert at working with children, but she figured that she could hardly expect a child to do something that she wasn't willing to do herself.

It just seemed reasonable that she would be the one who would have to get on Billy's back.

"Billy is actually quite tame," she said as she stood up, smiling with what she hoped was reassurance.

Despite the fact that her own stomach was writhing in anxiety and fear.

She had just barely gotten comfortable standing beside Billy and petting his head. The idea of getting on his back was...quite scary.

She could understand Chloe's hesitation.

But she had also put at least twenty other children onto the steer's back. She'd done it without thinking about whether or not it might be scary and especially hadn't thought about whether or not she wanted to do it herself.

How could she put all of those other children on the steer and expect them to be okay, if she wasn't willing to do the same thing?

Feeling a little guilty because she had expected young children to do something that she wasn't quite sure she was willing to do, she took a step back and made her smile grow even bigger.

"If it will make you feel better, I can show you how to do it." She was surprised at the confidence in her voice. Of course, after working at the newspaper for so long, she'd developed a bit of an ability to bluff.

She was using every ounce of that ability right now.

The little girl nodded her head, an exaggerated up-and-down motion which made her pigtails bounce like happy little blonde bubbles.

She was so sweet, and she tugged at Eliza's heart. Children had been something that Eliza had never thought about. She had been focused on her career, climbing a ladder, being successful, but... She wasn't even sure what her definition of success was anymore. Was it taking pictures of people who didn't want their pictures taken? Selling them to outlets where they would be plastered all over the world, against those people's will?

Of course, some people wanted to be famous. They wanted to be able to make money from their popularity and charm, so taking famous people's pictures hadn't felt like such an invasion of privacy.

But the line had blurred to the point where she didn't feel comfortable doing it anymore. As long as there was money in it, there would always be someone who was willing, but...that person wasn't going to be her. Not anymore.

"Are you going to do it today?" the little girl asked and not in a sarcastic way. Maybe just in a way that said that sometimes it took her a little bit of time to get her nerve up, so maybe it was taking Eliza a little bit of time as well.

"I'm sorry. Of course. You're just so cute, you made me think about kids and how much fun they are."

Of course, she wasn't so naïve as to think that children weren't a lot of work as well.

A *lot*.

Still, she wasn't going to have children without a husband. And a husband hadn't been even a remote possibility. Most of the men she knew were just as disinterested in families and children as she was.

It was kind of the new modern thing to just hook up but have no plans to actually get together in a permanent way, create a family, and nurture new little humans.

The idea was actually kind of scary.

But not quite as scary as getting on the back of the steer.

She looked at the mother of the little girl and held out her hand again. "I'm Eliza, and I'm not sure who you are."

"Jasmine. And I'm sorry. I should have introduced myself and introduced you to Chloe. I'm not used to adults getting down on her level and making her feel so comfortable."

"She's a sweetheart."

"Thank you. She is a little bit shy, and I appreciate you being willing to show her that there's nothing to be afraid of."

"Of course not. Billy's had dozens of kids on his back already today. But if you wouldn't mind holding him, not that I think he's going anywhere, just to let him know he's not supposed to." Hopefully her smile was hiding all of the nerves that were chasing each other around down in her stomach.

"Of course. I'm sorry. I should have offered."

"It's okay. This isn't like something that we're used to doing every day. At least I'm not."

"Me either. I'm just happy that Chloe has the opportunity. If you don't live on a farm, it's kind of hard to find cows to pet."

"I think for people who live on a farm, it's still hard. Sometimes."

Jasmine laughed. "That's probably true."

Billy wasn't that tall, and Eliza was pretty sure she could stand at his side, jump on his back so that her stomach was up over the top, and then swing a leg over.

Not that she'd ever done anything like that before, but that was her strategy anyway.

"Are you ready?" she asked Jasmine, on the pretense of making sure she was situated. But in actuality, Eliza was just giving herself a little bit more time. She wasn't sure, first of all, that she could get the whole way up on Billy's back. And then, she wasn't sure whether she wouldn't just fall off.

Then, there were the horns. They were huge. At least they seemed that way. And she didn't think that Billy would try to use them on her, but if someone tried to jump on her back, and she had horns that looked like that, she couldn't guarantee she wouldn't use them to at least brush the person off.

How could she expect Billy to be any different?

"Ready," Jasmine said with a smile, holding Chloe with one hand while her other hand held the lead rope that was attached to the rope halter around Billy's face.

She'd procrastinated enough. Eliza took one step closer to Billy and put both hands on his furry back.

He didn't move a muscle. His mouth kept going up and down, and he didn't even look around to see what was going on behind him.

She leaned a little of her weight on him, and again, he didn't move.

Taking a deep breath, she braced her arms, bent her legs, and jumped as high as she could, pushing with her hands, to get her stomach up on his back.

She did such a good job she almost did a head dive off the other side, and it took her a couple of seconds to catch her balance on his back.

Through all of that, Billy never twitched, as though he had people jumping on his back all day long every day and he was used to it.

Which was a good thing, because she needed the extra time to catch her balance.

She lay there over Billy's back, feeling like an idiot, with her head further down the other side than she was comfortable with.

Finally, after he didn't move at all, she pushed her torso up some while trying to swing her right leg over.

She felt about as awkward as she had ever felt in her life before and figured that there was probably a crowd of people standing around laughing at her, but as she straightened up, no one seemed to notice other than Jasmine, who stood with Chloe in front of her, still holding onto Billy's rope.

People mingled, laughing and talking, and the beautiful North Dakota fall sun shone down. Everything seemed to be going on as normal, and no one even stopped to notice that Eliza Walton, world reporter and city girl extraordinaire, was currently sitting on the back of a cow.

There should be trumpets playing or something.

She had no sooner thought that than Billy, who hadn't moved a muscle for the last two hours, casually took first one step then another, and then more as he moved away from the hay and pushed through the rope that had sectioned off his part of the petting zoo.

"Um, Eliza?" Jasmine said with just a little panic in her voice. "What should I do?"

"Can you stop him?" Eliza asked, hearing the same note of panic in her own voice. She had no idea what to do. She'd never...led a cow before. Was that what it was called?

"I'm pulling, but he's not stopping." Jasmine now had both hands on the rope, her daughter Chloe standing beside her with her fingers in her mouth. She had a worried look on her face, although Eliza only glanced back for a moment before she swallowed the lump that had clogged up the back of her throat and buried both hands in Billy's hair.

She wasn't sure exactly what to do, but she wasn't going to jump off, not while he was moving at a leisurely walk that felt more like a stampede, and she was hoping she wasn't going to fall off either. That was what the handfuls of hair were for.

"Stop?" It sounded more like a question. Like she was asking Billy if he felt like stopping today.

He gave the equivalent of a no, as he shook his head just a little, his horns waving back and forth, before he continued walking.

"I'm sorry, but I have to let go!" Jasmine said before she did exactly that.

Billy stepped out onto the sidewalk and casually, slowly moseyed up the street, like he normally took his human for a walk at this time of day.

Eliza, who had been in town for more than two months, knew it to be not true. She'd never seen anyone other than children sit on Billy. Why had she thought she should be the first adult to do so?

She felt trapped. She couldn't get off, she couldn't get him to stop, and she didn't know what to do.

Then, to her horror, Billy started to trot.

Trot, gallop, or something. He started to go faster, and her butt started to bounce. It wouldn't have been too bad, if she would have bounced in the same spot. But the problem was, every time she bounced she came down on a completely different spot, then bounced again, landing in a different spot, until she had bounced to the point her butt was sitting more on Billy's ribs than on his backbone, her leg over the side of Billy's back dug in, trying to hold on, while her hands that had gripped his fur pulled even tighter.

It felt like Billy was going like the wind on the sidewalk, but her logical mind told her he was a cow, and he wasn't going that fast.

Eliza didn't know what to do; she didn't want to fall off. And she didn't want to let go, and she was pretty sure that she wanted to stay calm and cool and collected, but she was pretty sure the scream that reached her ears came out of her own mouth.

She also was fairly certain that she was about to die.

# Chapter 2

"He needs someone to take care of him." Miss April sat at a craft table outside the community center. It was a beautiful day, and the Harvest Festival was in full force. She and her two friends, Helen and June, had a craft booth set up, somewhat apart from the rest of the festival, in the parking lot of the community building, where they usually resided.

People didn't have a problem walking down the street to check them out. The crafts were known for their superior workmanship, and they had quite a following.

If they had been sitting with the rest of the townsfolk, behind the diner, they would have sold out hours ago. What was the fun in that?

"No one is going to do it. And I wouldn't ask anyone to," Miss June said, shaking her head.

"I have to agree," Miss Helen said softly. "It's hard to want to ask anyone to take care of someone that you know is not going to be kind to them. But that doesn't negate the fact that he needs someone. And it seems to be our job to find someone." She sighed and bit her lip. "But I don't know who."

Miss April sat at her table, enjoying the short break from having any customers.

She had time to think.

Who in the world could they send out to Hines Cannon's house to take care of the disfigured recluse, who was known for his ill temper and antisocial personality.

He was also known for his rather impressive ability to tame the wildest horse.

Funny how a man who couldn't get along with people seemed to have some kind of gift for getting along with horses.

Still, Hines had broken his leg and needed someone to help him.

He was a bachelor, out there by himself, with winter coming on. She didn't know the specifics of whether he had enough firewood, fuel to burn for the winter, or money to tide him through or how he would get groceries.

He needed someone.

Someone who wasn't afraid to face down a man who was more than likely not going to be kind to them.

Someone who could meet him toe to toe and not be cowed by his bad attitude and grouchy, grumpy personality.

Someone who didn't have a job already and was looking to earn a little extra money.

Of course, then they would have to talk Hines into paying the person.

"We have our work cut out for us." She said it resolutely. They'd faced harder things and figured them out.

They could figure this out as well.

"I'm not sure that we're going to be able to accomplish it." June, being pragmatic, looked at her two friends.

Miss April nodded in acknowledgment. It was quite possible that this time June was right.

"We need someone brave." Helen fingered the edge of one of her quilted pot holders.

"Someone outspoken and bold," Miss April agreed.

"Someone who doesn't have a job, is willing to stay in North Dakota for the winter, and who will happily be mistreated and not murder the man in his bed. I don't think there is such a person alive," June said, shrugging her shoulders like that was that.

But Miss April didn't give up quite so easily. "I think we should pray about it. God just might drop someone right into our laps."

"That's more faith than what I have," Miss Helen said easily.

Something that sounded like galloping hooves drew their attention toward the east side of Sweet Water.

Miss April leaned over her table to get a better look.

It sure looked like Billy the steer, who was supposed to be in the petting zoo, had someone on his back and was galloping toward them.

Odd.

"That looks like an adult," Miss April murmured, picking up on an insignificant detail.

"I believe it is," Miss June agreed.

"I thought he was going to be in the petting zoo?" Miss Helen said, saying out loud the thing they all were thinking.

"What's an adult doing on his back?" Miss June murmured.

"Good question. That... That looks like my niece."

Eliza Walton, former reporter for the Houston World News and Reports, and a new resident of Sweet Water, had been living at her house. She hadn't gotten a job in Sweet Water yet, since she had been applying for writing jobs online.

Her dream had always been to be a writer, and she wanted to support herself with her writing even though she'd given up her reporting job, because, as Eliza said, she just couldn't stand to continue to profit over writing stories about people who didn't want stories written about them.

Of course, she still acknowledged the importance of having newspapers in the world, but it wasn't the kind of writing she wanted to do.

So, she walked away from what had been an illustrious and lucrative career. She had been on an upward trajectory and had been quite celebrated in her sphere.

But Eliza had fallen in love with small towns and with Sweet Water in particular.

Miss April couldn't be happier to have her beloved niece living with her. But she did worry over her some. After all, it was a huge adjustment for her city-raised niece to settle into small-town life.

Miss April lifted her brows at the steer who had settled down into a bouncing trot. Eliza, hanging off one side, bounced up and down over the sidewalk as the steer trotted along, looking as though she were going to fall off at any moment.

Case in point.

At least, as far as she was hanging over the side of the steer and as close as she was to the sidewalk, the fall would not be far.

Miss April and her two friends watched as Billy clambered to a stop, swerving at the last minute to miss Miss June's lunchbox.

The swerve was the final straw for Eliza, whose grip gave out, and she hit the sidewalk with a thump. Shoulder first.

Billy, just as calm as he always was, stood staring at them with limpid eyes, almost as though asking if they had any treats for him.

Miss April reached down for her purse. She had taken to carrying them around with her, after the second couple Billy had gotten together.

She was an aspiring matchmaker herself, and she felt like she needed to keep her friends close and her competitors closer.

Billy fell in the latter category.

"Good boy, Billy," she said, holding the treat out in her hand as Billy sniffed and then snatched it up.

"Good boy?" Eliza said, pushing herself to a sitting position on the sidewalk in front of them.

All three ladies leaned over their tables, looking around the steer to the woman whose hair hung over her face in disarray.

"Well, he did stop," Miss April said, not wanting to defend herself. Billy wasn't her favorite animal in the world, cows in general were rather annoying, since they stank, produced a lot of waste, and were rather clumsy. In her opinion, their only redeeming quality was that they tasted good.

But, again, Billy was the competition, and Miss April wanted to keep him in good standing.

"After he hauled me halfway across the town!" Eliza said, casting an irritated glance at the steer before she pushed herself to her knees, then clambered to her feet.

She winced, brushing at her shoulder and then looking at it.

"Looks like a brush burn," Miss June said, grabbing her purse and setting it on the table. "I have some things here we can use to take care of it."

"It'll be fine."

"Don't you want some antibiotic ointment?" Miss June said without looking up.

"No. I just want to take this steer, and give him back to the petting zoo, then go home and take a shower. I stink." She wrinkled her nose.

"I thought you'd signed up to be in charge of the petting zoo?" Miss Helen asked, her brows raised, as though that were a legitimate question.

"I did. But Billy ran off, so I think the petting zoo is canceled for today."

Miss April's eyes widened, and she tapped her chin. She had what she considered a really great idea.

"Can you cook?" she asked, trying to think back over the two months that Eliza had lived at their house. Miss April didn't really like to share her kitchen with anyone, and when Eliza had moved in, she'd been more than happy to allow her to do it.

"Not really. I can make a salad, as long as I get my chicken from the store," Eliza said, brushing off her pants and then allowing Miss June to take her arm and sit her down on the extra chair that they had set out just in case someone wanted to sit and visit.

"Did you take any nursing classes in college?" Miss April asked, figuring that she might as well. What were the odds?

"I went for journalism. Why would I take nursing classes?"

Miss April shook her head. "Can you clean?"

She hadn't had Eliza doing anything of the sort. Eliza went grocery shopping for her. Miss April would give her a list, and Eliza would bring back what she wanted. She did her own laundry, kept the door to her room closed, and had told Miss April that she would pay board.

Miss April had waved her off; after all, she was her niece, but now she wished she would have given her a job or two around the house. At least that way she would have known exactly what type of housekeeper Eliza was.

"You haven't been in my room lately, have you?" Eliza asked, lifting her lips in an almost smile. The first show of humor since Billy had dumped her at their feet.

"Why, no. That's your room, and I wouldn't go in without permission." Unless there was a very good reason for it, but Miss April left that little tidbit off.

"I work best when everything around me is in chaos. So, it's probably not up to sanitation standards, and if the town of Sweet Water were to inspect it, you might have a condemned notice tacked to your front door before the inspectors left."

Miss Helen, who had gotten quiet and seemed to have figured out what Miss April was thinking, lifted her head and met Miss April's gaze.

They shared a look before Miss Helen said, "She's perfect."

Miss April nodded her head. A decisive nod that left no room for any other opinion. "That's exactly what I thought."

Miss June, her head bent over the brush burn on Eliza's upper arm, froze, and then she lifted her head slowly and looked between her two friends. "You wouldn't do that to her."

"I think I would," Miss April said, her eyes narrowed, as she went through her mind, trying to think of any drawbacks.

She couldn't think of one.

"Do what?" Eliza asked, flinching as Miss June dabbed at her shoulder.

"I found a job for you."

"Well, that's great. I've been scouring the Internet and haven't been able to pick up much of anything. I do have savings, but I'd prefer not to use them."

Miss April shifted. She felt like she might have hit upon a great idea, but sometimes selling the idea wasn't her forte. She had a tendency to be a little pushy.

She knew it, she just didn't know what to do about it.

"Well, there is a man who lives outside of town, by himself, rather secluded," she began, thinking that was a good start. Eliza looked like she was listening, if not interested.

"He broke his leg," June said, pulling out a bandage from the little first-aid kit she apparently carried around with her.

What kind of person carried around a first-aid kit in their purse?

Miss April shook her head and continued. "That's correct. And he's not the kind of person who accepts help easily." How else was she going to say that he could be quite unpleasant?

Unpleasant wasn't even the proper word. Something a lot stronger. Mean came to mind. Eliza was pretty much fearless, but she didn't want to scare her away, just in case she'd been away from the city long enough to forget that she could hold her own.

Living in the country made a person stronger, but in different ways.

"And we're looking for someone who would be willing to help him out."

"I just said that I can't cook, I don't clean, and I took no nursing classes. I have no idea what to do with a broken leg."

"The leg has already been taken care of. He just...can't get around very well. He broke his arm, too, and he's in the hospital currently. He'll be released today or tomorrow." Miss April eyed her niece, trying to figure out what angle she could take that would talk her into doing what she wanted her to do. "I think you two grew up in the same town."

Maybe that would do it.

"Really? He's from Texas?"

"Houston, I believe. He used to be a firefighter there."

At that news, Eliza's brows went way up, and her facial expression went from casual to intense.

"He was a firefighter?" she almost whispered. "...How far out does he live?"

"Well, not many people have been to his house. He's a bit of a..."

"Recluse," June said, either not noticing April's caution or overriding it.

"He used to be a firefighter. And he's a recluse who lives around Sweet Water?" Eliza murmured.

"That's right." Miss April opened her mouth to try to break the news that he was the man who had rescued Eliza from the fire years ago and the man she had been searching for. It might be a shock. She needn't have worried.

"I'll do it."

# Chapter 3

Why had he come to the sale barn?

Hines Cannon looked around. It was a Monday morning, and he had expected things to be quiet.

When Miller had called and asked him to come take a look at a horse, he hadn't expected there to be people here.

He pulled his cowboy hat down low over his head and pulled up the collar of his coat, grateful for the cold that made it seem like a natural thing to do.

"Sorry. I didn't realize the buyers from Bismarck were going to stop in." Coleman, one of the few men in town he trusted, walked toward Miller and Hines, speaking low.

"Not your fault," Hines said. There was nothing to do about it.

"Just wanted to let you guys know. One of them brought his wife and family, so there are kids running around, too. I'll try to keep them out of your hair. Take your time." Coleman nodded to both of them, then walked off.

"Where's the horse?" Hines said to Miller, getting to the point and not wanting to get into a big discussion about how he didn't like to be around people.

Miller and Coleman both knew.

He could usually count on Coleman to be discreet.

Of course, not everything was under Coleman's control, and he understood that people could show up when he wasn't expecting them.

Still, that didn't mean he wanted to drag this out any longer than necessary.

"She's over here," Miller said brusquely, moving down an aisle with livestock pens on either side.

If Hines were whole, he would enjoy the walk. Enjoy the sights and smells, the sound of animals munching hay, the feel of the crisp wind that blew through the cracks in the slats on his face, the knowledge that winter was coming, and he was ready.

He loved the warm, safe feel of the sale barn. A place where men congregated. Where farmers talked about the weather and crops and the price of cattle, and where they shared their war stories. Stories of narrow misses, and some that didn't miss at all.

But the ones they lost served as a warning for the rest of them. They didn't hesitate to talk about them. To tell the stories of what had happened, how they were found, what they should have done differently. It was all laid out there. Laid out as a warning for anyone who thought that life on the farm was going to be easy. That there weren't going to be hardships. That farms were safe and fun.

They were. To a point.

Hines didn't have any war stories from his farm.

He could tell one from his firefighting days.

That wasn't so much of a warning though. He would do it all again, exactly the same, if he had a chance.

Just... It had made living the rest of his life more difficult.

But he followed safety protocols to the best of his ability and had only broken them in order to save a life. If he hadn't, a young woman would have died.

"I put her back here, because I thought it would be best to keep her away from people as much as possible."

Miller spoke over his shoulder without slowing his stride. Hines could feel the skin stretching on his legs where the scar tissue from the burns pulled as he lengthened his stride. Walking was not as painful as it had been immediately following his accident, but it would never be comfortable again.

Not this side of heaven.

Still, Miller was a childhood friend and one of the few people in town who knew what his face looked like. He kept up, ignoring the pain.

Instead, he put his mind on the horse.

The corner they'd walked to was darker, the light bulbs spread out more sparsely.

There weren't any animals in the stalls they passed; this area seemed to be used only when the sale barn was exceptionally busy. Maybe for a holiday sale or something special.

Regardless, Miller stopped in front of the last stall in the corner. Hines had to squint in order to see over the boards and into the almost pitch-black interior.

There was hay in the rack and a tub of water in the front corner.

But the horse wasn't eating hay and wasn't standing by the water.

She didn't neigh when they stopped, or walk over, looking for treats or wanting to be scratched.

Instead, she cowered against the far side, her ears pinned back. Clearly saying, as emphatically as a horse could, that if they got within biting distance, they could expect to lose a finger.

But it wasn't the horse's posture that made Hines's soul groan.

It was the way the ribs poked out, standing out in stark contrast even in the dim light.

He could count each rib. See the hip bones jutting out, see the neck that despite the complete lack of nutrition was still gracefully arched.

The head, with not an ounce of extra fat on it, still held elegance and class.

"How did you get her in here?" he finally asked, seeing that their presence was agitating her to the point where she not only had her head back, but she kicked against the back wall, almost as though she were hoping to knock it down to escape.

"We had to drug her. Lark gave me some meds. Enough for two. That's what we'll have to do to get her on the trailer. Even then, she was hard to handle."

Hines didn't say anything to that. He'd figured as much. If she had just come in today, the effects of the drug probably still hadn't completely worn off, and she still looked ready to run or fight. Whichever was necessary.

"I have some good Samaritans who saved her off the meat wagon out by Chautauqua," Miller said, naming a town an hour or so to the west. "They couldn't handle her but couldn't stand to see her go. She's...got so much fight left."

No doubt. As his eyes adjusted to the dim interior, Hines could see the scars that littered her thigh. Or maybe they were just patches where her hair had fallen out because of poor nutrition, he wasn't sure.

His heart twisted.

Some thumps and a commotion from the other side of the barn drew the horse's attention from the people in front of her as she perked her ears and lifted her head, looking over them.

Hines didn't pay attention. The sale barn was always active and busy when there were people around, and usually there were animals constantly running around. As secluded as this area was, though, he wouldn't need to worry about seeing anyone.

Miller knew how he was, and the secluded spot was perfect for the horse who obviously didn't like people either.

"She'd be gorgeous if she had more weight on her," he murmured.

"Yeah. I'm not a horse person, and even I can tell that."

Miller said he wasn't a horse person, but he'd been working with horses for several years. Just because he hadn't grown up with them didn't mean he wasn't good with them. Hines figured Miller probably loved horses just as much as he did.

"I like your spirit," Hines murmured.

Her eyes flashed, and she continued to hold her head high, even though she was so weak he could see her legs shaking.

"I really don't know much about her. The Helpful Humane Horse Association rescued her, but no one could work with her. They didn't want to take her back to the kill pen, but they didn't know what else to do with her."

"I assume that they've been feeding her, and she was probably in even worse condition when they got her."

"I'm sure. But they didn't have her for very long. She...was considered a danger to the help. They were afraid someone would get hurt and authorities would come in and try to shut them down."

That made sense to Hines. It also made sense as to why they were asking him to take her. She was too beautiful, with too strong of a will to live, to be put down.

"Can't tell what her coloring is," Hines said, squinting closer. Not that it mattered.

"She's a blue roan. Gorgeous coat, even with the scars and shag."

Hines nodded. That kind of coloring would make her expensive, even without the breeding information. Most likely, she had no papers, or even more likely, she had papers that had been lost over time.

"She's too weak right now to hurt anyone, but I know when she gets stronger, she's going to be a handful. Deuce could tackle her, but he's busy right now with his wife and just moving back to Sweet Water. You're the first person I thought of after him."

"He's not too much into rehabbing horses. He's more into training them."

Miller nodded in agreement, and they didn't say anything more for a while, just looking at the horse with her ears pricked, her head lifted, her eyes wide.

This one definitely needed some rehabbing.

But Hines could relate to that. He could also relate to the scars on her coat and the fact that she would never look the same as she used to.

He had the same scars, not just on his legs, but all of his torso, and they had disfigured his face.

Surgeries had made it a little better, but he still looked nothing like the person he used to be.

Nothing like the way a normal person looked. The horses he worked with didn't care.

"I'll take her."

He really didn't need to think about it. The first moment he laid eyes on her as she stood in the back of the stall, scrunching there, trembling, he couldn't have done anything else but his very best to try to rehabilitate her and bring her back to the land of the living.

The settlement that he'd gotten from the accident had ensured he wouldn't have to work again for the rest of his life.

He'd given half to his sister, knowing that she would prefer him over the money but hating that just his being with her brought teasing, taunting, and negative attention. It had just been the two of them growing up in foster care, but he'd given her half the money and then he moved from Texas to North Dakota, finding a place that was as isolated as it could be.

That had been ten years ago.

He hadn't talked to or seen his sister since. He missed her, but he always knew it was for the best. People couldn't stand to look at him, and she would have to deal with it. He didn't want that.

He refused to allow his mind to dwell on the things he left behind.

Suddenly the horse whinnied, and Miller jerked beside him. Hines realized the commotion had gotten a lot closer. As he jerked his head up and looked down the long corridor, he realized three cattle had gotten loose from somewhere and were running toward him.

After a second, he realized that a child, maybe elementary age, ran in front of them screaming.

Possibly someone who didn't know anything about animals was chasing the cattle from behind, causing them to continue to chase the child who ran ahead of them.

"I'll get the kid," he said shortly.

"I'll get the gate," Miller said with words just as clipped.

Hines did not need to be told that Miller was going to open the gate on his side and try to get the steers to run in while Hines grabbed the child and pulled him to the other side.

Stepping forward just a bit and unlatching the gate of the pen just up from the pen the horse was in, he waited another couple of seconds for the terrified child to run to him.

Maybe it was his imagination, but the kid seemed to run faster once he saw Hines standing there, seeing him as a rescuer.

The cows weren't exceptionally large, and they didn't have horns.

Probably they would have executed their rescue attempt with no injuries, except Hines grabbed the child and shoved the gate in, shoving the child into the pen, intending to run in after him, but his old injury gave his stride an ungainly limp, and he tripped, falling forward into the pen, pain shooting up his arm.

Thankfully, the kid had moved into the pen far enough that he didn't fall on top of him. But his legs were still out in the aisle.

That wouldn't have been a bad thing, except one of the steer's legs caught on his and ripped it ahead, only as far as the side of the opening of the pen allowed. Then his leg caught against the corner.

The pressure from the steer pushed forward on it, creating a lever, and Hines felt intense pain before he heard his bone snap.

It only took a few seconds, then a multitude of people followed the steers down the aisle, which ran right through the gate Miller had opened, heading into a pen, and Miller closed the gate behind them.

Hines assumed all that, because he lay on the floor, his entire consciousness red with the pain that radiated out every pore.

"Are you okay, mister?" the kid said, standing up and brushing himself off.

"Yeah," Hines ground out, balling his hands into his fists, giving himself just two more seconds to lie there praying that the sharp, almost unbearable pain would settle down into a dull throb. Into something that he could stand for the length of time it was going to take to get him to the hospital.

"I'm calling an ambulance. There is no doubt your leg is broken," Miller said, his words low and floating down, but they still hit Hines's ears like bullets. Probably because his entire body felt unbearably sensitive because of the pain in his leg.

He didn't even bother to argue. There was no way he was going to set a bone like that. He couldn't see his leg, but he'd be willing to bet it was lying at an odd angle which was why Miller had known immediately it was broken.

Going to the hospital was the last, the very last, thing he wanted to do, but he wasn't going to have a choice.

"Still want the horse," he ground out.

"I never doubted that," Miller said. "I'll get her to your house, and I'll make sure she's cared for until you're back."

"Thanks." He was probably going to need someone to care for her for longer than that, but he wasn't going to make those arrangements right now. Miller would see to it and would care for her until he was able to take over. If he couldn't do it himself, he'd at least pay someone who could.

He had a housekeeper, Alice, but she most likely was not going to add caring for his horses to her list of duties.

"I've got other horses to feed," he said.

"Don't worry about it." Miller's words were confident and said in a way that did not allow for any kind of argument.

That was the best kind of friend to have. One who came through for a person when they were down. Hines was most definitely down.

# Chapter 4

Hines shifted uncomfortably.

He had only been home for an hour, compliments of Miller, and already he was stir-crazy.

Of course, spending fourteen hours in the ER while they x-rayed his leg, decided on a treatment plan, and then realized he'd cracked a bone in his arm as well hadn't helped anything.

They'd wanted to keep him for another day or two. They'd also wanted to send him to a specialist.

He refused both, and maybe because the hospital was in North Dakota, and they were used to men who refused to do what the doctor wanted them to, or maybe they took one look at his twisted and angry face and knew they weren't going to get anywhere with him, they didn't argue further.

Instead, they had the orthopedic doctor on call cast his leg, put his arm in a sling, give him some pretty good pain medicine, and then they sent him home after making sure that there would be someone there to take care of him.

He had assured them that there would be, conveniently leaving out the fact that his housekeeper, Alice, only came on Mondays and Fridays.

As long as he didn't move, it didn't hurt.

Even if he never moved, he was pretty sure that he'd be hungry eventually.

Thankfully there were meals in the refrigerator.

Alice came, cooked three or four meals, did some light cleaning, and picked up any groceries he asked her to.

He figured that counted well enough for the doctor.

Miller had told him when he dropped him off and helped him get settled in a recliner that he'd already unloaded the horse in the paddock and would make sure she had feed and water every morning.

Hines had assured him that he would be able to take care of it in the evening.

He wasn't sure whether that was true or not. But there was something about the horse that had called to him, stirred his heart and soul.

Of course, he loved horses, always had, and had helped several dozen of them since he moved to North Dakota, but this one felt different.

He couldn't wait to get a good look at her in the daylight.

It was frustrating to be laid up when he wanted to get started on caring for her and taming her down right away.

Of course, he knew that with horses in general, one had to take it slow, and with a horse like her, that was extra important.

He shifted again, pain shooting up his arm and down his leg. He gritted his teeth in frustration.

It wasn't like he'd never been laid up before.

*Lord? Why does everything seem to happen to me? Isn't anything good ever going to happen?*

He knew that was a negative thought. He was blessed to be able to live in North Dakota. Surrounded by beautiful country. A state that wasn't highly regulated, and he was free to do many of the things he wanted to. His house was small but paid for, and his farm had plenty of acreage for the horses he cared for.

God had blessed him with a gift. A gift of patience and intuitive knowledge of what a horse needed in order to be rehabilitated.

Not everyone had that, and he was grateful.

*Sorry, Lord. I guess I get testy when I'm in pain. I know You've been good to me. Thank you.*

The one thing he wanted was someone to share it with. A wife. Someone to walk through life with him.

But since his burn accident, he knew that would never happen. No one wanted to be with a man who looked like him.

He had to push that thought aside, or he would sink back down into depression.

He spent a lot of years in that ugly place where he felt like the world was against him and nothing good was ever going to happen.

Considering that he had a broken arm and broken leg and he was going to be laid up again, it was going to take everything he had to keep from wallowing in self-pity and bitterness.

With that thought, his doorbell rang.

He looked around for his crutch. It lay against the far wall. Which meant he would have to get out of his chair and hop across the room in order to get to it.

He hadn't even considered asking Miller to move it closer before Miller had left. He wasn't used to being down. He'd thought that part of his life was over.

Wincing from the pain, he leaned forward, shuffling ahead in his seat as the person at the door rang the bell again.

"Come in. It's open," he hollered, figuring they probably wouldn't hear him through the heavy wooden front door.

But the handle clicked, the doorknob turned, and the door pushed in.

His jaw clenched as the face of a young, pretty woman peeked around the door before her body came into view.

She wore jeans and a flowing shirt that was the same emerald green as her eyes. Her hair fell in soft waves around her shoulders, and she moved with a gracefulness that, to his chagrin, drew his eyes and made it difficult to look away.

He had his share of experiences with beautiful women after his accident.

They made him feel inadequate. They also made him feel bitter because he would never be considered handsome again. It shouldn't bother him, because he knew that looks were only a surface indicator and did not indicate character or integrity, but it was also true that humans seemed to be hardwired to want to look at beautiful things.

He certainly couldn't deny the fact that he wanted to just gaze upon this woman.

Then he shook himself.

He didn't recognize her. What was she doing in his house?

"What do you want?" he asked, the question coming out more gruffly than he had intended. Not just because she was pretty, but because he had spent the last ten years or so of his life avoiding people for this very reason. They made him uncomfortable.

"I'm here to take care of you." The woman's words were soft but not scared or unsure. She said them firmly, and she wasn't asking for his permission.

"I didn't ask for anyone to come take care of me."

He almost said "and I don't need anyone either," but that wasn't exactly true. He hadn't managed to get out of his chair, and his crutch was the whole way across the room.

It was going to hurt a lot for him to hop to the other side of the room to get it.

Although, ninety-nine percent of him wanted to do everything on his own, without any help.

"I didn't say that you did," the woman said, closing the door behind her, softly, with what felt like a very decisive click.

But her movements were not short or in a hurry. They were casual, like they were friends somehow, and she was just walking into his house the way she had done a hundred times before.

Unsettling.

"Stop right there." He kept the panic out of his voice but just barely. He didn't want her coming any closer.

She stopped obediently, but while the expression on her face was not unsure, she lifted a brow in inquiry as though she were simply waiting for him to say what he needed to say before she continued on. He hadn't realized she was carrying a grocery bag. He noticed it now. It rustled softly as her movements stopped and it brushed against her leg.

He didn't know what to say. *Leave?* He wanted to.

"Who sent you?" he asked instead. "I don't know you."

That last bit was said almost as a question. After all, she was acting like they did know each other. Comfortable in his house, walking toward him like they were friends, smiling a little, and here to...take care of him?

"Does it matter?" she asked, and there was a little bit of humor in her voice. Which was melodious and gave his heart a stir every time he heard it.

"Of course. You could be here to steal everything I have."

"Yes. I've been searching the completely empty countryside high and low for a house to rob." She said that with a heavy dose of sarcasm, and he almost smiled. After all, if a thief were looking for a house, they really would have to search in order to find his. Surely there were easier pickings in other areas.

"If I'm a thief, I definitely need someone to give me lessons, because there's got to be an easier way to make a living than roaming North Dakota trying to find a house with a man who has a broken leg and broken arm who can't stop me when I try to steal everything he owns, which...no offense," she said as she looked around, "doesn't look like much from the outside."

He bristled at that, even though he knew it was true. His house was modest, deliberately so. His settlement had been tens of millions from the accident years ago, and he'd spent very little of it. Buying this farm, buying a couple of horses, and buying hay over the years when his farm hadn't produced enough for him to feed the stock that he had.

Most of the money was in investments which Miller had been managing for him. Miller's father had been an investment banker, and while Miller hadn't followed in his footsteps, he'd helped his dad as a part-time employee the entire time he had been in high school.

Hines and Miller had been best friends, and even though Miller had been in the military when Hines had gotten burned, he'd come around to visit. When Hines had told him about the settlement, Miller had offered to invest the half that remained after he gave some to his sister for him.

Miller had been going to do it for free, just because they were friends, just because he wanted to do something to help his buddy, but Hines hadn't wanted to hear that. He paid him. Not just because he could, but because he deserved it. If Miller hadn't been around to help him with his money, he might not have had any. As it was, his money hadn't doubled in the last ten years, but it made enough in interest that he could live quite comfortably on it.

Still, Hines wasn't going to make it easy for the woman, and he allowed his irritation and offense to shine through in his words. "It might not look like much to you, but it's home to me."

"If I were a thief, I wouldn't have chosen this place to rob. That's all I was saying. I think it was a compliment." The woman narrowed her eyes, as though thinking back on her words and trying to make sure she wasn't saying something that wasn't true.

"I don't think it was."

"I'm the one who said the words. I can tell you what the meaning was behind them. You can only guess."

His mouth clamped closed. She was right. That was true about anything. He couldn't discern the thoughts of any man or woman. He didn't usually have someone in front of him telling him that though.

He wasn't going to give up on their argument that easily.

"And I'm the only one who can tell you how I took them."

Her lips quirked up just a little more, and she inclined her head.

To his chagrin, he felt his lips trying to imitate hers. He wanted to respond in kind to her humor and good nature. Interesting that she hadn't even seemed to notice the scars on his face and the way it was misaligned.

The rest of his body was the same. Although all that he could cover was hidden with long sleeves and long pants. His hands were a little scarred, and if he were out in public more, he would probably practice hiding them. As it was, he didn't spend any more time out in public than he had to. In fact, aside from his trip to the auction barn to look at the horse, he hadn't been out since last Christmas, when he'd gone in late to the Christmas Eve service, stood in the back listening to the beautiful music, watching the lights, seeing the heads of the happy people, and listening to the sermon, before slipping out as the closing hymn played.

Christmas was when he missed his sister the most.

"You're right about that. I apologize if you misunderstood my meaning. I certainly did not mean to give offense."

He wanted to say he took offense anyway, but the woman seemed so friendly and nice that he just couldn't bring himself to be mean or rude.

"Forgiven," he said begrudgingly. "That doesn't change the fact that I didn't ask for anyone to come take care of me."

"Perhaps the reason that you didn't open the door yourself was because your crutch is sitting across the room from you? Perhaps you can't get out of your chair and walk to it because you have a broken leg and you're not supposed to be on that leg? Perhaps it's going to be hard to walk anyway, because your arm is fractured, and you can only use one crutch."

"Someone's been telling you about me."

"You don't need to sound so offended about it. Sweet Water is a small town, people talk. And they care about you. That's why I'm here. Because someone cared enough about you to think that you might need some help beyond your housekeeper."

She even knew about Alice. He gritted his teeth. She was right. The town was right. And while it irritated him on the surface level, there was a part of him that felt warmed and cared for, noticed the way all humans longed to be noticed, cared for that the town would think that he needed someone.

"Who's paying you?"

"I didn't talk about payment when they asked me to help. They just said there was a need, said someone needed me, and so I came."

She was hiding something. She dropped her eyes for just a moment, and he could tell that there was something else she was fighting not to say.

"That's not the only reason," he said, not knowing what it could be but knowing there had to be something else that would have made her come out here.

"Really? You wouldn't hear that there was something in need and go help them no matter what? A horse, for example?" she said, her lips working a bit again, like she knew about the horse he'd just rescued.

He finally said begrudgingly, "Thank you. I try to make sure they are." His eyes narrowed. "Are you a reporter?"

He had inquiries over the years. People who wanted him to do interviews. To talk about the fire and his experience, supposed heroism, and scars.

He hadn't wanted the attention. Especially with the way that he looked. Reporters always wanted pictures to go with their stories.

His question made her uncomfortable. She shifted. He figured that would be one reason she would jump at the chance to take care of him. The reason she would do it without pay.

"You are," he accused. "You're a reporter. That's why you're here. That's how you know so much about me. You've asked questions, the way a good reporter does." There was no compliment in that last sentence. "That's why no one is paying you to be here. You'll get money from the story when it runs. You can leave."

His voice hadn't risen, and there was no anger in it, just a controlled dislike.

He'd hated reporters since his accident. They had been persistent. Taking pictures as he walked around the hospital in his gown. When they hadn't been able to get anything else to splash on the front page, that was the picture they ran. A little fuzzy circle covering the gaping hole in the back.

Irritating. Frustrating. It made him angry. Like his pain didn't mean anything except a good story.

Of course, they really wanted the story because of his supposed heroism, but he hadn't done anything that anyone else wouldn't have done. Any other firefighter would've done the exact same thing. He didn't deserve credit for doing something that anyone would have done. He just had the opportunity. And he took it.

Of course, it meant saving a life.

"You are partially right," she said, her tone a little softer, a little less confident. An apology in it.

"I thought so." He wanted to show her the door, but he couldn't even get out of his chair.

"I used to be a reporter. I do know the questions to ask. But I quit." The word sounded final. A little sad, like she'd left her job but had quit for a reason that had given her no other choice.

"I don't believe you," he said, even though that was mostly a lie. He could tell from the tone of her words that she really had quit. Of course, maybe she had quit because she couldn't make any money at it, and she had decided that the story about him would be just the thing to break her into the business again. He could see that happening.

"It's true. I chose to quit. I chose to come to Sweet Water where my aunt lives. I moved in with her, and I was looking for a job. I do love to write. I'm not going to deny that. And I also keep a journal of what I do during the day. My thoughts and feelings about it. I just... Writing is something that's a part of me. I can't just give it up. But I have no intentions of writing a story about you and publishing it."

"Why should I believe that?" he snarled. The snarl was because he actually did believe it, and he didn't want to. He was irritated with himself for falling under her...spell? Or maybe just because she was beautiful, she could manipulate him into doing whatever she wanted. It had been a long time since a beautiful woman had a conversation with him.

All his fault. Since he didn't go out, he didn't come into contact with any beautiful women.

"Because it's the truth." Her words were simple, accompanied by a little shrug of her shoulders, which made the bag at her side rustle again.

She tilted her head, looking at him, somehow her look reminding him that he was still sitting in his chair, his arm and leg both killing him, with very little hope of getting out without a lot of pain.

"Please let me stay. I... I owe you."

What in the world could she mean by that?

# Chapter 5

E liza walked over to Hines's chair and held her hand out.

"I'm Eliza. It's good to meet you." She almost added "finally" onto that, but she didn't.

He hesitated, staring at her for a moment.

Her heart thumped in her chest. Her breath caught in her throat. Suddenly her mouth felt dry, and she wanted to sit down.

Would he question her about her name?

She could see his teeth gritting, his eyes narrowed like he was considering his next words. Or maybe trying to remember something.

Eliza was not exactly a common name, and he might ask about it. She held her breath. Part of her wanted him to. To get their connection out in the open.

Part of her suspected that if he knew who she was, he would refuse her help.

Of course, he might refuse her help anyway.

"Eliza. That's not a common name," he said, his hand moving, then stopping, almost as though he were reconsidering, then slowly his arm lifted up, and his hand clasped hers.

It was big, rough, and scarred. Partially deformed, from the scars that pulled at his skin. It wrapped around hers, warm and confident.

She blinked, not expecting to have so many emotions roiling through her with a touch of his hand.

She schooled her features carefully, shaking it, while he continued to look at her with questions and suspicion.

"You saved my life," she finally said.

"So it is you."

"Yes."

He jerked his head up, almost as though acknowledging her words, but he didn't say anything, and their hands separated again, hers falling back down to her side, feeling...alone. Which was an odd way for a hand to feel; she had wanted to continue to keep a hold of his. She couldn't recall that ever happening in a handshake before.

"I can't even tell," he finally said, after his eyes had roamed over her face and down her arms. He looked at the rest of her too, but not in a lewd, uncomfortable way. "I thought you'd been burned."

"The scars are on my legs. I can show you if you want." She hoped he didn't take her up on it. Her pants would have to come down from the top, since the legs were too narrow for her to pull up from the bottom.

He shook his head. "I don't need to see them. Mine are on display for the world."

"I'm sorry. They're my fault."

"I never blamed you. I do have trouble wondering why God allowed that to happen to me, but I don't blame you."

"If it hadn't been for you deciding to come in and get me, I would have died."

"I know."

That was true. After the explosion in the school kitchen where she had been having a home ec class, she had been knocked unconscious and trapped under a heavy...beam? She wasn't sure. She just knew that when she came to, she was alone, there was fire everywhere, flames, heat, and she couldn't remember where she was. She was scratching through her memories, scared to death because she couldn't move, and calling for help.

"I couldn't be sure I even heard a voice. When I chose to go back in, I didn't know whether it was to save someone or just to satisfy my conscience that there was no one left behind."

"You didn't hear me call?"

"I thought I did, but I wasn't sure. No one else heard it, and that almost convinced me that I was making it up. That I had some kind of... I don't know, death wish or maybe hero wish."

"Hero wish?"

"I think sometimes as a firefighter, the idea that you save people goes to your head. You want to prove that you're a hero. I don't know. I never really thought I felt like that, but when no one else heard anything and thought I was crazy for going back in, in fact, I was told not to, I thought that maybe I was just making something up so I could win accolades."

"Maybe it was the Lord prompting you. Knowing that I needed someone, that I would die without you doing what needed to be done."

"Yeah. That was probably it. But at the time, I doubted myself."

"If no one else heard a yell, I can see why."

"They never did. No one ever said that they heard you calling for help. I... I couldn't even have said it was a human call. I just heard something."

The conversation seemed to make him uncomfortable.

"Do you have nightmares?" she asked, wondering if it was the bad memories stirring in his heart that made him shift and seem like he wanted to talk about something, anything, else.

"Not really. Sometimes I dream I didn't get to you in time. But the nightmares are never about me, they're about not saving you."

"I always wanted to meet you. I wanted to thank you in person for what you did."

He changed her life. Made her understand the price of heroism, that sacrifice wasn't always guaranteed, and sometimes men didn't do their jobs.

Sometimes they did.

She'd written about that for years.

"Obviously I'm not much to look at," he said, meeting her eyes with a gaze that she could only call fierce. Like he was staring at her to disagree with him and somehow say that wasn't the truth.

"I wouldn't be here if it weren't for you." That was an easy answer. And the truth.

"Well, now you found me and said thank you."

She cut in before he could say anything more, because she highly suspected he was going to show her the door.

"Yeah. I know. So now I can get to work." Her tone became brusque, like she was shrugging off the bad memories and focusing on the task at hand. "You can tell me where the kitchen is, and I'll start making lunch for us." She lifted the bag she held in her hand.

"Ah. That is where your sources are not quite accurate. Alice makes me lunch. I have meals in the refrigerator for the week. She will come back on Friday and make them for the weekend."

"All right. Then I'll make something for myself. And if you happen to like what you smell, I'll share."

She didn't wait for him to say anything more, but turned, walking toward his crutch, picking it up and bringing it back, leaning it against his chair, where it wouldn't be hanging over his head but would be within arm's reach if he needed to get up.

There were a lot of things they could talk about having to do with the fire. About what happened to him afterward, maybe even her, if he was interested. But now did not seem like the time. She had not gotten to the point where he was accepting her and agreed that she should be around, helping him. That was her first goal. After she'd achieved that, then she'd worry about whether or not they would ever discuss what happened after he rescued her.

About her scars. And his.

"I understand you're not supposed to get up, unless you have to use the restroom. I'll leave this here, assuming you're going to follow the doctor's orders." She lifted her brows at him, not in a condescending way but not in a questioning way either. She wasn't going to give him authority over her. So she was just saying it as a matter of fact. The same matter-of-fact way she gave him a small smile and then walked through the living room, turning right into the kitchen.

"I never said you could stay," he called after her.

"I don't recall asking," she threw back over her shoulder, keeping the tremble out of her voice and setting the bag down on the counter with an internal sigh that she did not allow to escape from her lips. She didn't want him to know that she was concerned he would tell her to go.

She wanted to help. She wasn't kidding when she said she owed him. She owed him her very life. Taking care of him while he was recuperating was just a small price to pay.

From what her Aunt April had said, no one else was doing anything.

Of course, there were a lot of people in Sweet Water who didn't even realize he lived here.

"If you're going to stay, you can bring me a glass of ice water and the TV remote."

She laughed, going immediately to get him the ice water he asked for and walking into the living room. She wasn't going to ask if this meant he was okay with her staying. She was just going to make that assumption.

She smiled as she handed him the glass. "Do you mean to tell me that someone left you in here with the TV set right in front of you and no remote? That's like some kind of form of torture, isn't it?"

He didn't quite grin, but his eyes twinkled. "Miller's been my best friend my whole life, but his idea of a joke can be a little harsh."

"All right. You let me know when Miller comes to visit, and I'll bury cayenne powder in his serving of dinner."

"He never eats here," Hines said, the smile on his face gone, his eyes turned back away from her. Like he didn't want to get too close by joking and having a conversation with her.

Maybe those were the kind of walls he put up between him and everyone else. To keep himself safe.

She could understand that.

She looked around the room, her eye catching on the remote that lay on the stand under the TV.

She walked over, got it, and handed it to him without a word.

"Will it bother you?" he asked, without looking at her.

"Probably not. If it does, I'll just go outside."

"You can't take care of me, be my nursemaid, if you're outside."

"I'm not going to be your nursemaid. Just so we're clear about that. I... I thought I would come, stay for the day, and leave once you're settled for the night. I'll...help you get in and out of your chair, fetch things for you, and anything else you want me to do. I understand you have some animals who need to be fed?"

"I see. You have experience on a farm, and you can feed and water them for me?"

"If you tell me what to do, I'm pretty resourceful, and I'm not afraid of work or of new things. If that's what you're insinuating."

"I have a horse here that killed a man. They were going to put him down, and I rescued him, not without a lot of trouble. You think you can feed him?"

Was he challenging her?

He did a good job if he was. Fear ripped through her chest. A horse that killed a man?

"I don't think the horse is a monster. You're still alive," she finally said, not knowing how else to respond to that. Maybe it was a warning.

"Because I know horses. Because I'm careful. Because—"

"I can be careful too. And I trust you. You didn't save my life all those years ago, just to send me out to a killer horse now."

"Maybe I have changed. Maybe I've gone over to the dark side."

"All right then. I guess that's a chance I'll have to take. I'm not worried about the horse, and as long as you're taking care of me, I'll leave my life in your hands. You did a good job with it when I was fifteen. I'm going to assume you'll keep doing a good job."

"Assumptions aren't always a good idea."

"I feel safe with this one."

They stared at each other for a moment. Eliza wasn't exactly sure what they were saying. Whether any words passed between them or not. Maybe it was just a challenge, to see who was going to back down first. He wasn't going to make this easy on her. She'd figured that out already. Even if he did have a connection to her, even if he had saved her life, he wasn't going to just accept her.

He was known as a recluse, and there were reasons for that.

She hadn't come here thinking she was going to save the man, just help him. But maybe there were a few things she would be able to help with, beyond his broken bones.

She could only hope that God would give her the wisdom to help him heal his broken spirit as well.

# Chapter 6

H ines sat in his recliner, morose.

In the kitchen, Eliza hummed softly to herself while pans and dishes clinked and clacked as she washed them in the sink.

Since his accident, he hadn't seen a lot of people. He hadn't been very welcoming, and he had only been as friendly as necessary to the people that he had to associate with.

He felt like he was justified considering how he looked.

This was the first time he felt guilty.

Maybe it was because Eliza was the girl he rescued. He always wondered what happened to her. He had declined all interviews, requests for comments, and any attempts at reaching out to discuss the incident at all.

He hadn't gone back in to be a hero, despite what he had told Eliza about wondering if he had gone in, imagining someone calling to him, just to get that hero status.

He figured anyone in his profession probably dreamed of being the one who saved the day, but he also knew that they would just do what needed to be done, because that was their job.

Still, just in case there was any kind of lingering need for him to have some kind of weird glory, he had refused everything.

Well, that, and because he was grossly disfigured.

All the plastic surgeries he had since his accident had not been able to turn him back into the person he had looked like before the accident.

He finally gave up the plastic surgeries, telling his doctors he wasn't interested anymore.

Maybe, if it had been up to him, he wouldn't have had them to begin with. But he'd agreed because that was what the doctors recommended.

He didn't regret them necessarily, just...just hated the way he looked. But he would hate it if he hadn't had the surgeries.

The fire, being a hero, had ruined his life.

The humming continued, although the clanking stopped. He could picture her moving gracefully, with those smooth movements that he'd admired all day.

Unobtrusively of course.

Eliza had absolutely made his day much nicer. He couldn't imagine what it would have been like if she hadn't been there. She had brought his crutch, for one. Although it had been extremely painful to go to the bathroom, he'd done it. She brought his pain meds at the proper times, fluffed his pillows, brought him an extra one, and adjusted the stool for his foot. She'd done his laundry, even though he protested when he'd seen her with his clothes basket, and somehow, he wasn't sure whether it was because she had cleaned, or just because she was there, but his house smelled better than it had in years.

Yeah. He should probably tell her not to come back.

It was almost seven o'clock. He was pretty sure she'd be going home anytime. This was his opportunity to make sure that she didn't interrupt his life again.

Except, he didn't want to.

He turned his head as she walked into the living room, a fresh glass of ice water in her hand. And a pitcher in her other.

"I assume you're going to sleep on the chair?" she asked, striding in with the same confidence she displayed all day. Not overt, she didn't swagger or stomp, but rather an understated person who knew their worth and didn't worry about what other people said about them.

He liked that, admired it.

"Yeah. I'm not going to attempt to get down the hall, just to come out tomorrow. I'll stay here. At least until it stops hurting when I breathe."

"I can't believe they didn't make you go to rehab." She set his glass down, picking up his old glass which was still half-full but all the ice was melted and the water was warm. She set the pitcher down beside it.

"They wanted to make me. I refused." He also said he had someone helping him at home. Which was true if he counted Alice.

"Well, I'm sure they were doing that for your good. The doctors do have a tendency to know what they're talking about. Not because they've experienced it, necessarily, but because they've watched what other people have done and gone through."

"And they can be wrong at times too. I will get much better, much faster, much happier here."

She straightened, his old glass in her hand, her eyes looking down on him. "I believe that."

"I want to apologize to you." He hadn't planned on saying that, he thought he'd catch her as she was walking out the door. Apologize and tell her not to come back.

"For what?" she asked, looking surprised.

He figured she should know.

"Because I wasn't exactly welcoming when you walked in today."

"You weren't expecting me. That's fine. You warmed up to me fast enough." Maybe there was a little bit of humor in her tone, because he hadn't really warmed up to her at all. He appreciated what she'd done, but he hadn't told her that.

He hadn't allowed her to know that he was thankful for what she was doing at all. In fact, if anything, he'd almost gone out of his way to be irritated with her.

That's what he was apologizing for. He supposed she was going to make him spell it out, since she refused to say that he hadn't been the kindest.

"You know I owe you an apology."

"You do not. You could have been really rude. And you understand that I wasn't exactly nice to you when you were rescuing me out of the fire. I don't really remember much, other than I was scared of you, fought you, although I was grateful that you were there at the same time. It was the head injury, I think."

He remembered. She'd screamed in terror. Probably at the fire suit he wore.

He'd been terrified too. Although, she probably hadn't been able to tell. But he hadn't been entirely sure they would get out. In fact, he'd been pretty sure they were both going to burn to death, and her terror was justified.

The only thing he could say to explain it was that God had shown him the way.

"I have been very appreciative of the things you've been doing. I'm grateful that you're here. You...were a good help when I needed to use the restroom. I don't think I could have done it without you. And you kept up with the pain meds. That's been a real help too."

"How is your pain?"

"It hurts."

Getting his mind off the pain by thinking about her all day had helped with that. Of course, she was beautiful, and who wouldn't think of her?

He was under no illusions that she was thinking the same about him. Just grateful that he had saved her all those years ago and here to pay it back. That irked him some. He didn't want to be just an obligation on someone's list they were checking off.

Of course, there wasn't much that was likable about him. His personality had soured and become a reflection of his looks.

All his fault. He had allowed it to happen.

"Are you leaving?"

"I'll stick around for a little bit. I assume you probably don't go to bed until ten or so. I'll help with at least one more trip to the restroom."

He grimaced internally. As much as he appreciated her help, it was embarrassing as well.

"I'm sure you have things to do."

"I've sat at the table and done some of the things I have to do," she said.

He had seen she went out to her car after lunch was over and brought a briefcase back in. She had her laptop set up on the table, and she asked for his Internet password.

He provided it, and they hadn't talked any more about it.

"Is there something on TV you'd like to watch?" she asked, her eyes roaming around until they landed on the remote. It sat behind the lamp on the table next to him.

"I never watch TV. I don't even know why I have one. The thirty minutes I spent watching today was more than I've watched since last winter."

The documentary on World War II airplanes would have been extremely interesting for Miller. As it was, Hines had watched with a modicum of interest, but it couldn't hold his attention. He'd rather be out doing things than watching other people do them.

"I am not much of a TV watcher either. Would you...like for me to sit and we can talk?" She looked at the chair that sat at an angle beside him.

He hadn't meant to get two chairs, but when he had gone to the estate sale, they had been sold as a pair. They were the only recliners in the sale, and he hadn't wanted to move heaven and earth to furnish his house. So he bought them both.

"Sure. I don't know what you'll talk to me about though." He wasn't much of a conversationalist. He was very rusty.

"Well, we have our hometown in common."

"Texas. What are two Texans doing in North Dakota?"

"That's a good question."

"Actually three, because Miller's from Texas as well."

"Miller's here because of you," she said easily.

"Actually no. Miller went to the Air Force, and I ended up becoming a firefighter. I feel a little bit bad about that, because Miller wanted to do the same thing, but they only had one opening, and they hired me."

"That could destroy a friendship."

"True, but it didn't. Miller's bigger than that."

"Well, that's good for him, because some men aren't."

"I know." He was quiet for a bit, realizing he had been blessed in his friendship. He didn't often think about what a great friend Miller had been over the years, but it was true. He supposed it would be better for him to have a good friend than to have a handsome face.

That was a thought he hadn't had in a very long time, if ever. Interesting that Eliza seemed to bring that out in him.

"I had some friends or at least people who told me that they were my friends, who ended up not being friends."

"That's too bad."

"It had to do with the fire and my scars, I think. They would never say it."

"What scars?"

"I'll show you some time," she said. He found himself wondering why he had to wait. But he didn't say anything. Still, he wouldn't turn the offer down. He wanted to see how badly she'd been burned. He would have guessed she was worse than him, but he was the one the world could see. Looking at her, he couldn't tell.

Then again, it had been her legs that had been next to the fire.

"I think they were embarrassed to be seen with me. Maybe not in school, because people were used to me there. But when we went out, shopping or something. I mean, you know Texas gets hot in the summer, and I would have looked ridiculous if I had been running around with jeans on. People stare at my legs. I took to wearing long skirts, but even so, they still bring attention to you. I...didn't exactly fit in after that."

"I see. I didn't realize."

"Not in a bad way. I guess it just showed me who my friends were."

"Things like this usually do."

"Yeah." She lifted her chin a little, as though bracing herself to say something hard. "I've always loved to write, but I had been hoping to have a career as a model. I had been scheduled to go to New York City that summer for a two-week invitation-only modeling camp."

"You lost a career in modeling because of your scars?" He hadn't known. His stomach dropped, and he felt like he should apologize for that, even though it wasn't his fault.

Interesting, that she had lost so much too. But she didn't seem to be bitter or angry about it.

"I don't know. It was promising. I had been chosen out of tens of thousands of girls across the United States, so there was that. But modeling is notoriously competitive, and who knows what would have happened. Maybe the fire saved me from something that I might have regretted, either in New York City, physical danger, heartbreak. I don't know."

"You never experienced heartbreak?" Why he zeroed in on that, he had no idea. Normally he didn't talk about things like that at all.

"Not really. I was married, just for a couple of years. He...decided he'd made a mistake and walked out. I didn't really get a choice about that, and although I was devastated at the time, I can see that I felt like the marriage was probably a mistake, and he was right. I just... I would have stuck it out anyway."

"Because you're not a quitter?" he said, maybe a little sarcastically. That would be the only reason most of the world would give to stick with a marriage that was less than ideal.

"No. Because I made vows. They meant something to me."

He agreed but didn't say anything, feeling bad that he had given her a jab about not quitting. Of course. A person needed to keep their vows.

"So you don't regret or resent the fact that you couldn't be a model?" He assumed that the scars were what kept her from it.

"No. I never pursued it. Maybe I could have been anyway. I've never seen anyone with scars as a model, but...different body types are being used more and more. Maybe I could do it. I just... I realized I didn't want to. I was actually kind of grateful for the fact that the fire kept me from pursuing a career that I think would have made me miserable. Or at least it would have changed me into someone I don't want to be. But often, we don't realize that we're becoming someone we don't like, and we end up liking who we become, and we have a fundamental shift in our character that enables us to think that who we became is who we wanted to be all along."

"Or we just love ourselves so much that whatever we become we embrace as well."

Ouch. Even as he was saying that, he knew it applied to him. He had become bitter and angry, and he had allowed himself to become that. Encouraged it. Told himself that he deserved to be able to be mean, and it was what he could expect, because of what he'd been through.

But looking at it through the shift that Eliza's words caused in his head changed his mind.

"I guess... I guess I spent some time resentful that I wasn't perfect anymore. Or at least perfect in the way the world considered me perfect. But the fire wasn't my fault. I was doing exactly what I was supposed to be doing. And God is in control of my life. I believe that, right? So He allowed that to happen. I don't know why, but I knew it was for my good. So I tried to start thinking I needed to let go of what I thought my life should look like, my expectations, and embrace it for what it is. Love each day for what it is, and not expect it to look a certain way that suits me rather than God."

Maybe it was the fact that she'd been there all day, the fact that she was a ghost, so to speak, from his past, or maybe it was this new injury that brought out everything he thought God owed him. But her words hit him like a brick in the forehead.

He wasn't appreciating his life for what it was, and he was disappointed it hadn't turned out the way he thought it should.

He was resentful and bitter.

"It's kind of funny that we had very similar experiences, and you came out with such a different mindset than what I did."

"I have to thank my parents for that. They were older, so maybe they were wiser, but they didn't allow me to sit around and mope and wonder why. They pointed out people who had it worse than I did. Who couldn't walk or talk or had other problems, and there I was, complaining about a few scars. They really didn't let me wallow in my self-pity."

"That stinks. I had a really good time wallowing."

She chuckled a little, and his lips wanted to turn up in a grin, but he didn't let them. He didn't smile. He never smiled. He supposed his eyes were probably twinkling though, because they crinkled, and he couldn't help it.

He wanted to laugh with her.

Maybe the feeling would pass, or maybe he should tell her not to come back. That way he wouldn't have to worry about whether or not he had that feeling.

"I wanted to have a good time wallowing too. But my parents said once I got down in the pit, it was going to be a really hard thing to climb back out, so they told me to set my sights on my goals and dreams and plans, and work to achieve them, but to not get so sold on the idea of needing to have what I wanted that I wasn't able to adjust course when God clearly wanted me to. I suppose, having a beam from the ceiling fall down on you is a pretty big wake-up call."

"Being burned over half of your body is another big wake-up call," he said, but the comment didn't come out as lighthearted as he meant it to.

It was a wake-up call that he had hated. He hadn't thought, *maybe the Lord is trying to tell me something.*

Or maybe, he stumbled into it anyway. Since if he hadn't been burned, he probably would still be back in the fire department in Texas. He wouldn't be in North Dakota, wouldn't be rescuing horses, wouldn't be living a life that he loved. Except, the lingering bitterness and anger had clouded most of his interactions. But why? He was happy here. He enjoyed it. Other than possibly wanting a wife and family, God had given him a really good life.

"I just realized I wouldn't have this life if it hadn't been for the fire."

She smiled at him, like the knowledge wasn't surprising to her at all, but she was proud of him for figuring it out.

Automatically he started to get upset about that, but then he calmed himself. He shouldn't be upset, he should be thanking her for pointing out the things he hadn't seen and hadn't taken the time to think about.

He hadn't quite gotten to the point where he wanted to thank her, but he didn't have to get upset. And he wouldn't.

"You know, a lot of times the bad things that happen to us in life are just things that open up doors for other people or situations to happen. Things we wouldn't have if we hadn't had the trial to begin with. I suppose that's really what made me decide that I needed to start letting go of my expectations of how my life should be. You know, like I have the expectation that I should live my life without any scars on my legs. And that's not going to happen. They're never going to look the way "normal" legs look. I can accept that, let go of my expectations and just accept the fact that that's the way it is. And then, it's my job to do my very best with the life that I have in front of me. Not getting upset about the things that happen, accepting them, and realizing that it's my part to do my best with what's left."

He sighed, laying his head back against the chair and closing his eyes.

"I'm sorry. I didn't realize you were getting tired. Pain always makes me exhausted."

He nodded his head and didn't open his eyes. It wasn't that he was so tired, it was that he just realized he'd wasted ten years of his life.

Not wasted. He couldn't look at it as wasted. That was ten years that he had behind him to help him learn a lesson. The lesson being he could only change today, he couldn't change the past, so there was no sense in being upset about it.

What she had said about accepting her life the way it was made so much sense that he could hardly believe that he hadn't done that for himself.

"I'm coming back tomorrow. I was here at ten o'clock this morning, but only because I knew when you were getting home from the hospital. I figured I'd probably show up around six?" She grinned a little. "I don't want to get you out of bed, but I also don't want to miss you getting out of bed."

"You don't need to be here from six in the morning until ten at night every day."

He leaned his head up and opened his eyes.

Looking at her was not a hardship. He loved her smile, loved the way she moved, and loved the way she thought. That her thoughts challenged him to change his thoughts. Or maybe, her thoughts were just lining up with what the Lord wanted him to think anyway. Regardless, he probably should just tell her to stay away. But he couldn't.

"Whatever time you get here will be fine."

"What time do you usually get up?"

"Usually I'm up by five, sometimes a lot earlier. I feed the stock and take care of them before breakfast, then I work with them."

He wouldn't be doing that for a while. It felt like forever, but he was old enough to know that six to eight weeks would be over before he knew it.

Still, living through them would feel like a long time.

"All right. I'll be here at five."

"No. I was saying, that's what I usually do. I won't be getting up and feeding any stock. Miller is coming, and he's going to take care of everything for me. He'll probably stop in before he goes out to the barn, or after. So I'll be okay. You can sleep in."

"I'm a morning person. Actually, I'm a night owl, but I want to be a morning person, so I've been changing my thought processes. I think of myself as a morning person. I think morning is a time that I love. I think how much I enjoy seeing the sunrise. I don't allow myself to drink caffeine after noon, and I don't take a nap after that, either. I deliberately give myself things to do so I'm out of bed earlier than what I normally would be. I said all that to say you would actually be helping me learn to do something that I wanted to do all my life but have never been able to."

"Interesting. I... I just have animals to take care of, so I get out of bed. It's not really that big of a thought process for me."

"Not everybody is as blessed as you are."

She winked when she said it, and that time, he smiled despite himself. He would never have considered himself blessed. But when she said it, it made him believe it. And she was right; he really was blessed. Blessed to have animals who got him out of bed in the morning. Blessed to be out to see the sunrise, even if it was frosty and cold, those were beautiful sunrises too, along with the summer sunrises, where he could look at the sun in a T-shirt and feel the breeze over his skin, and just be so grateful to be alive.

"I don't think about it that way, but you're right. I am blessed."

She nodded, and they sat there in silence for a while. He was startled, several hours later, out of a light sleep when she stood from her chair.

"I'm sorry. I was trying to get up without waking you."

"No. I wanted to know when you were leaving."

"Now. I'm heading out. Would you like me to help you up to use the restroom before I go?"

He shook his head. He could wait until morning. He didn't want that to be the last thing she did before she walked out. Maybe it was a pride thing, but regardless, he waved her off.

As she opened the door, he said, "Thank you."

She had no idea that he wasn't just thanking her for her help today. But thanking her for opening up the door of his mind and letting him think that maybe things weren't as bad as what he thought they were.

# Chapter 7

Hines was awake the next morning when Miller knocked on his door. The perfunctory knock before he opened it and walked in.

He could tell from the rap that it wasn't Eliza. It was powerful and short, a knock that said *you don't have to answer, I'm coming in anyway*. Not a knock that said *hello, is anyone home*?

He kinda laughed because he shouldn't be able to tell the difference, but it was easy.

"Good to see you're not dead yet," Miller said as he walked in.

"Good morning to you too, sunshine," Hines said, not the slightest bit surprised that Miller walked right by him and straight to his one-cup coffee maker.

The cupboard door opened, coffee mugs rattled, water poured out of the sink, and Miller didn't say anything until he came back into the living room with two steaming cups of caffeine.

"This is how I know you are a good friend," Hines said as he took the proffered cup.

"Because I know how you like your coffee?"

"Because you know not to talk to me until you hand me a cup."

Miller snorted and blew a little on the liquid in his cup before he took a sip. "I guess that means you're a good friend to me too."

They didn't say too much as they drank their coffee together, Miller standing in front of the big picture window, looking out at the sunrise, Hines in his seat at an angle behind him, watching it too.

There wasn't much to see, just a lightening of the eastern sky, but Hines never got tired of watching it for some reason. The start of a new day and all it represented. The amazing idea that every morning the sun came up the same. That it could be ninety-three million miles away, so much space between them, and he'd never actually touch it with his fingers, but that the heat touched his face, and the light and energy it gave provided everything the earth needed in order to sustain life.

God's amazing ability to create such a vast and impressive network that ran perfectly, with nothing, at least nothing to the naked eye, holding it together, and yet they could predict down to the precise second the moment the sun would break the horizon.

He didn't always think such deep thoughts when he watched the sunrise, but it always stirred his soul. Made him aware of his Creator, and the power and omnipotence of God, made him feel small. Not in a bad way, but in a way that amazed him that God, despite his smallness and seeming inconsequence when he pictured the universe, still loved him. Loved him so much that he would die in order to save him.

The thought boggled his mind.

"Heard you had a visitor yesterday."

"Other than you?"

"I'm not a visitor."

"You're a thief." He smiled a little at the memory of Eliza saying that she wouldn't have searched all over North Dakota only to settle on his house as the one she wanted to rob.

"Really?" Miller shook his head. "After putting up with your grumpy rear for our entire lives, all you can do to thank me is to call me names. Take another drink of your coffee, because you need it."

"Actually, I'm in a pretty good mood this morning. Even without the coffee." And he found that to be true. Maybe it was because of his conversation with Eliza yesterday. It had opened his eyes. He was in charge of his future. He was the one who got to decide to accept his life the way it was and make the best of it. Dwelling in the past, and the negativity of the "if only that would have or wouldn't have happened," was pointless.

In fact, any sentence that began with "if only" was a pointless sentence and an even more pointless and futile thought.

In the end, he'd lived in "if only" too long. Even if he had only articulated it to himself.

The sunrise represented a new day, fresh and clean, with endless possibilities. That's the way his life was. If only he saw it that way. What was in the past didn't have to shape how he saw his future.

"Because of your company." Miller's words interrupted his musings, and he had to think for a moment before he realized that he was talking about Hines being in a good mood because of Eliza.

"I almost told her not to come back."

"But you didn't?" Miller said immediately.

"No. But I was tempted to."

"Because you liked her too much." Miller didn't have any problems reading between those lines.

"Why don't you make yourself useful and help me get to the bathroom." Normally he wouldn't ask for help at all, but he'd been holding off going, because for once, the pain in his arm and leg were both just slow throbs, and he didn't want to stir them up.

"Put your arm around my neck, and I'll carry you over," Miller said, sounding resigned, although Hines knew he was messing with him.

"Just hand me my crutch."

Eliza had left it right by his chair when she left, but he'd knocked it down during the night and hadn't leaned over the chair to get it, since even though it wasn't on the side of his broken arm, it would jiggle his leg.

Miller didn't say anything but walked over, set his coffee down on the table, and got his crutch. He helped him stand, and while

Miller was capable, and he didn't worry about falling, he kind of wished he'd waited until Eliza was there.

"She smells a lot better than you do," Hines said, causing Miller to grunt with a laugh.

"I can push you back in your chair, and you can wait for her to come. She is coming, right?"

"She said she'd be here by six. Which is why I wanted to get the bathroom trip over with."

"Even though she smells better?"

Hines didn't say anything, focused on moving. He supposed a bedpan would have been the smarter way to go, but he just couldn't do that. Well, he could if he had to, but as long as he was capable of mobility, he was going to make his way to the restroom.

Miller had him settled back down in his chair before he said anything more. Picking his coffee cup back up and looking out the window again at the changing sky.

"I think it's going to be a good one today."

"The sky is good for it," Hines had to agree. Sometimes the sunrises were so beautiful they almost brought tears to his eyes. And sometimes they seemed almost understated. He loved them all.

"Any special instructions?"

"You know to be careful of Grizzle." Hines didn't really need to remind Miller about Grizzle. Miller had been around the ranch long enough to know that while Grizzle wasn't really dangerous, it was still smart to keep an eye on him. He hadn't killed a man by trampling him, but the man had been trying to ride him, and Grizzle had reared and gone over backward. The man had been crushed, and although he lingered in the hospital, he hadn't made it.

Grizzle hadn't been a terrible horse, but his reputation followed him and he changed hands a few times, losing weight and being poorly treated, until he'd fallen in with Hines.

"What about the new one?"

"You put her in the corral, right?"

"Yeah."

"If you just make sure her trough has water, and she has hay, that should be good enough. I don't want to start her on feed until she gets settled here. She shouldn't need anything else until I'm able to get out. I... I don't think she'll be mean, but you never know."

"Yeah. And my expertise is airplanes. Horses... I like them, but sometimes they don't like me a lot."

"They like you. They just have trouble showing it."

Miller rolled his eyes. "I've heard that girl's been looking for you. Just figured I'd warn you."

Hines nodded. It made sense that she'd been looking for him, since she was the one he saved all those years ago. But the fact that she was a reporter was probably what Miller was referring to, and Hines couldn't deny that that concerned him as well.

"She came here with the paparazzi when Kenni came."

"She was with the paparazzi?" That was news. Hines hadn't known. She told him that she quit.

"Yeah. I guess she and Kenni are friends now, but that's who she came with. And her aunt, Miss April, has made no bones about the fact that her niece was a big-time reporter. Guess she's won a bunch of awards and crap like that."

"I see. She didn't mention that."

"Didn't figure she would. I'm not saying she's not here because she wants to be a little do-gooder, I'm just saying she might have ulterior motives. And I figured I'd warn you."

"Thanks. I knew she was a reporter. But she told me she quit."

"That's a recent development then, because it wasn't that long ago that Kenni strolled into town."

"I know." He got all of his news from Miller. Most of it anyway. Every once in a while, he had to go in town, or chose to, like at Christmas.

But he never got any gossip.

"Oh. Did I... I mention to you about Billy?"

"Billy?" Hines asked, trying to figure out where in the world he'd heard that name before.

"The Highland steer that hangs around Sweet Water."

"The one you tried to tell me was a matchmaking steer?" Hines laughed. "Yeah. I remember Billy."

"He's out beside the paddock with your new horse."

"Think he's matching himself up with her? I thought you said he was a steer? And he's a cow. I'm sorry, someone needs to tell him she's not interested."

"You need to get a name for her. And I'm not worried about Billy and your horse. I'm worried about you. Billy started his career by matching people together in town, but the last few times, if he shows up at your house, you're pretty much done for. I'm just saying."

"Well, Billy is going to have to bring a girl here—" His sentence broke off abruptly. There already was a girl here. She was arriving this morning, after spending the entire day with him yesterday.

"Exactly. I...kind of think Billy might be screwing up on this one. You don't need to be falling in love with the reporter who is trying to write a story on you and out you in whatever ways she's trying to do it. Just stuff you don't want."

"Thanks. I... Maybe I'll have to have a chat with Billy once I get up and around."

"He works pretty fast, so I'd be careful if I were you."

He wanted to laugh. He wanted to laugh so much, but unfortunately, there was some truth to Miller's words. Enough truth that instead of making him want to laugh, he figured he probably ought to start crying.

# Chapter 8

Eliza hummed as she slowly crept down the stairs of her aunt's Sweet Water home.

She wasn't a morning person. She hadn't been lying two weeks ago when she told Hines that she'd been trying to develop into one.

Part of that effort was making herself be happy in the morning. Hence the humming.

For the most part, it worked. When she got up, she didn't allow herself to think about how tired she was or how she wanted to stay in bed longer. Instead, she tried to focus her mind on all the things that would be happening that day and how happy she was to be alive and enjoying life.

Even if it weren't that exciting. After all, she'd been doing the same thing for two weeks every day. So she could hardly call it exciting, but still, she tried to convince herself that she looked forward to each day. Looked forward to what the Lord had for her and tried to make the best of it.

Today, she put on a knee-length skirt. Up until this point, she'd worn jeans. Today, she decided that she would talk to Hines about her scars.

It was no coincidence that today was also the day that Miller and his friend Gideon would have finished the ramp they were making for Hines.

They were working on it last night when she left, and Hines hadn't said, but he was excited.

After the first day, he seemed to be a little bit more standoffish. Less likely to smile and talk. He'd apologized for his gruff manner, and he wasn't rude, just...not friendly.

She had to assume it was because he didn't want to get too close to her. She heard that that was something that he was concerned about. As a recluse, it was probably the reason he'd gone into hiding to begin with. And she could respect that.

So there really was something to look forward to today, walking around the farm pushing his wheelchair. He could get in the chair himself, but he couldn't push it because of his broken arm.

She didn't want to be late and have Miller already out with him, when Miller needed to feed the animals.

She knew that was just an excuse. She wanted to be the one to push Hines around. She wanted to see the farm, and having Hines out on his wheelchair was a great excuse. He kept talking about his new horse, and they'd been throwing some names back and forth, but he wanted to see her before he named her for sure.

"You're happy this morning."

Eliza gasped, her hand going to her throat. "Oh my goodness. You scared me."

"I know. I'm sorry. I'm not usually up this early. But I wanted to see you." Aunt April sat in the dim kitchen, her Bible open in front of her, although Eliza couldn't say for sure how she saw it, since the light was so bad.

"I'm sorry. I've been gone since before five each morning, and I come back late."

"I guess he needs a lot of help."

"I suppose. Or company. No one comes to see him, and I think he wants it that way, but at the same time, surely he's lonely."

"I imagine so." Aunt April nodded. "Is everything going well?"

"I think so. I'm enjoying it. He seems a little standoffish, but I think it's just because of his nature. That's what drove him to become a recluse in the first place."

"Maybe because you're a reporter? Surely he knows that by now."

"Yes. But I told him I'd quit. He doesn't have any reason to not believe me, and it's the truth."

"That might make him nervous."

"It might."

"I heard Billy's out there."

Now that was a loaded question. She'd heard about Billy's reputation around town. Actually, her friend Kenni had told her that he truly was a matchmaking steer. She said she spent less than five minutes beside him, and she ended up married.

When Eliza saw Kenni again, she could let her know that she spent the last two weeks petting him at least once a day, and she wasn't any closer to getting a ring on her finger than she had been before she started. Not that she wanted one. Although, if she did, she'd like to have someone just like Hines. Without the reclusive tendencies, of course.

While she wasn't an extrovert exactly, she definitely didn't want to be cut off from all people and only shop in town once or twice a year.

Even with that, he was a great person. Just...not willing to let her in. Which grated some, but she understood.

"He is. He's a great steer. He loves to be petted, and I even got Miller to bring out treats from the feed store. He loves them."

"You know what that means?"

"Well, that's what it's meant for other people, but not for me."

"No one ever thinks something is going to happen to them. And then it does."

"But I'm different. Billy can't match me with anyone. I've got a mind of my own." She said that without a whole lot of arrogance. Maybe a little. After all, she did pride herself on not allowing other people to tell her what to do. She made her own decisions. And a Highland steer certainly wasn't going to affect that in any way.

"I heard Hines is a pretty good man. If you can get beyond the facial scars."

"You know, I noticed them the first couple of days we were together, but after that, it kinda surprises me when people talk about it, because I don't see the scars when I look at him. I see...a man who wants to be better."

So many people she knew were content with themselves the way they were. Were content to be angry or would say "that's just the way I am. I've always been short tempered, and I'm never going to change." Or "I'm just a bossy person." Or "I always look at the negative side. I call myself pragmatic."

She loved that Hines could see that he had faults, and instead of just not caring, he wanted to be better. She admired that.

"So there is someone under there? Someone worth knowing?"

"Yeah. He...was a hero in his hometown. Maybe someday he'll tell the story to Sweet Water."

"You could tell it. You're good at writing."

"No. That's not my story to tell." She had been keeping notes about her visits. Not because she wanted to tell Hines's story, just because she always kept notes. A little journaling in the evening, sometimes even in the morning. Her thoughts and opinions on things. Notes about how the day went. She supposed, more and more, her notes had been filled with Hines, but that made sense since she was spending every day, all day long, with him.

"Has he paid you?"

"Yes. He actually asked me who was paying me, and I told him I didn't know. I felt like it wasn't really fair that he had to pay me, since he wasn't the one who hired me, but it didn't seem to matter to him. So yeah. I got one paycheck last Friday, and tomorrow I'll get another one."

"That's pretty big of him. Considering that it wasn't his idea to begin with."

"I know. I appreciated it. Although, I do have my small savings, so it wasn't like I needed it."

"But you couldn't take another job while you're doing this one."

"True."

Although she had put her computer up on the table and taken a few small writing jobs. Nothing major. Nothing that would keep her from giving him her very best. He deserved nothing less.

"You have a skirt on," her aunt said, just now noticing her bare, scarred legs.

"Yeah. I... I thought Hines might want to see them."

That maybe didn't come out the way she meant it to, but her aunt understood, nodding solemnly.

"I think you two might be good for each other," she finally said.

"I think so. I know he's been good for me. I... I enjoy talking to him. He listens to me, which is not always true in people."

"I agree. Sometimes you run across people who don't seem to hear a single thing you say. They never seem to pay attention. And you end up being friends with them, and sometimes you wonder why."

She had a few friends like that. "That isn't Hines. I think he remembers everything I say. It's almost a little unsettling how much he remembers."

"Maybe he's interested in you."

"I hardly think so. He puts up with me because with his broken arm, he really can't get around very well. In fact, I haven't seen you to tell you, but his friends Miller and Gideon were making a ramp for him. Today he should be able to get out of the house and get around and see his animals. I'm really looking forward to that picking him up and giving him a boost."

"I'm not sure I could stand being in my house for two weeks."

"You know, he really hasn't gotten short tempered either. You'd have thought he would."

"He probably just sits and watches TV all the time."

"He doesn't. That's what's so surprising. Sometimes he'll have a documentary on when I get there, and sometimes we'll watch something in the evening, but most days, he reads books and talks to me."

"Kind of rare to find a man who talks to you. Maybe you want to snatch him up after all."

"I'm not interested. I have too many things I want to do with my life."

"Thought you were coming to Sweet Water to settle down."

"True." But she hadn't come intending to get married. She had come hoping that she would get to meet Hines. She had no clue that she would actually end up working for him.

But it wasn't a job that was going to last forever, and she really didn't know what she was going to do when it was over.

"Do you get a day off?"

"I haven't asked for one. I'm sure he would tell me I could. And his housekeeper comes on Mondays and Fridays. But... I don't really want one."

That was probably crazy. She would miss him if she wasn't there. Sure, it was a job, but he was more than that to her. She was getting to know the man who saved her life.

If it weren't for Hines, she would not be breathing right now. She wouldn't have had the last ten years to work and live and enjoy.

And because of what he did for her, his entire life had been changed. She couldn't give him his life back. Couldn't change it. And she shouldn't want to. Whatever had happened to him, God had allowed.

She didn't feel any misplaced guilt, but she did...want to know him.

Of course, about that, she was drawn to him like she had never been drawn to anyone before. But that wasn't something she was going to act on. She couldn't. He'd been very clear that he wasn't going to allow her into his inner circle. Even if he was going to be kind to her and treat her with respect.

"If there's anything that I can do to help you, just let me know. You've been working long hours. If you're not taking a day off, I feel like I should reach out and give you a hand. If I can."

"Thank you. I appreciate it. Maybe, if I talk to Hines and he's okay with it, you can come sit with him while I run some errands in town. There are a few things I need to do, things that aren't time sensitive." She needed to get stamps at the post office, and she needed to buy some pens. She also wouldn't mind talking to Kenni a little and finding out if she knew anything about Hines.

"I better get going. Today's the day the ramp will be finished."

"Take care," her aunt said.

She went out the door, humming again.

# Chapter 9

H ines sat in his chair, watching headlights flash across the barn before they stopped and then shut off.

He smiled. Despite himself.

He had heeded Miller's warning. He was not a naturally trusting person, although Eliza with her easy smile and calm manner would be an easy person to trust. Still, he knew she could just be out for the story. And he had been careful not to give her anything else as fodder.

He just couldn't bring himself to tell her not to come back though.

He thought Miller would be happy if he had, but Miller hadn't been on him.

He knew his friend only wanted the best for him and was trying to protect him from any more heartbreak.

Still, he couldn't stop the jumping of his heart as she walked up the walk and opened the door with a perfunctory knock.

He grinned, liking that she felt so at home in his house.

"Today's the big day," she said in a greeting.

"I've been looking forward to it. They wanted me to take a spin last night, but I told them I was going to wait for you."

Her eyes brightened a little at that, and while it made him happy, Miller's warning was loud in the back of his head.

She closed the door, and that's when he realized she wore a skirt.

Since they talked the first day she'd been there, they hadn't mentioned her scars again.

He figured when she was ready, she might show him. But maybe she'd never be ready.

"Your legs." That's all he could think of to say.

She turned, her hand still on the doorknob, her eyes, blinking a couple of times, staring at him.

"I was thinking to myself that it feels like you won't let me in. Sure, you're nice to me, and sometimes we laugh a little, but you have a wall between us. Which is fine." She lifted her chin and looked away, and he got the feeling that she said it was fine, but it really wasn't. "And then I realized that your scars are out for me to see. At least some of them."

He had a lot more that she couldn't see. But they weren't any worse than what showed on his hands and face.

"And you don't know mine. Not that it matters, it's just...something that makes you feel vulnerable."

"Yeah." He knew all about feeling vulnerable. It felt like that every time he went out in public. People looked at him and thought he was some kind of monster. He made children cry. He embarrassed his sister. He didn't think he would ever get over that.

Except, he had to.

He had decided that he was going to accept every day as it came. And not have expectations. He couldn't do that if he was constantly thinking about what he didn't have.

"So here are mine."

She kept her chin up as she walked forward, slowly, from the door to the middle of the living room where he could clearly see her legs, which were not shapely the way a person would think they would be by looking at her face and torso. Surprisingly skinny, like the muscle had never grown back, with the skin pulled and stretched the way burn scars often were.

"They're that way almost the entire way up to my thigh. I look...pathetic."

"You look like you survived something really hard," he finally said. But he supposed he could be talking to himself. There was nothing he could say about her burn scars that she couldn't say right back about his. How could he offer her comfort when he refused to accept it himself?

"That's right. I survived. Thanks to you," she added, nodding in his direction as though giving him credit for that. "What was the point in surviving if I'm going to let my scars define me? If I'm going to let them hold me back from the things I want to do? I'm not going to."

"You're not modeling."

"Because I decided I didn't want to. And that's the only reason. After being in the hospital for so long, you know how painful it was, how the days dragged, the infections, the isolation, the boredom. You know all about it."

Boy, did he ever.

"I didn't want to be vapid. Having people look at me just because I looked good in clothes. Because my face was beautiful or whatever. I had plenty of time to think in the hospital, and that's not what I wanted to live my life for."

"So you became a reporter instead?"

She wanted to know about walls. Right there. That was why he had walls.

"I wanted people to know the truth. I wanted to put the truth out there, because so many reporters have the truth, then spin it so that it goes in their direction. I didn't want to spin. I wanted the straight truth."

"That's how you ended up in the paparazzi chasing Kenni around?"

He thought she might be getting the idea, because her eyes narrowed some. Then she smiled a little as though she were on to him.

"No. I came chasing Kenni around, as you say, because I knew you were here. I took that job, just because I wanted to come to Sweet Water. I never turned down a chance to come here. Because I knew that's where you were. Or that's where I'd heard you were."

He couldn't say anything about that. She might be telling the truth.

"I don't think they usually let people who were reporting real-life problems go on the entertainment beat." He didn't really know anything about reporting, but if someone was reporting news or political things, they didn't typically do entertainment too. He was pretty sure about that.

"I asked. Kenni was a very lucrative assignment, and I was a good reporter. They let me go."

They stared at each other, and he wondered what in the world was going on in her head. Why she was looking at him like that. Had she figured out why he held her at arm's length?

"So that's why you don't trust me?"

Bingo. "Am I right to be suspicious?"

"No." She didn't hesitate, but she didn't elaborate either.

"And I should just take your word for it?"

"You can take it however you want to." There was frost in her tone. Like his pushing had finally made her step back. He didn't like the gulf that lay between them now. And it was all his fault.

He pushed out of his chair. It took a while, although he was better at getting up than he had been. One arm and one leg made movement difficult, but he'd had two weeks to practice.

When he was finally standing, he pulled his T-shirt over his head.

He wasn't sure why he did that. Maybe because she had been brave enough to show him the scars that she could easily have kept hidden, he figured he'd show her the ones that he had. Even though she'd already seen the ones he couldn't hide. It wasn't like a person could go around hiding their face without attracting even more attention, although he'd been tempted to do so.

She didn't even blink. He supposed after seeing his face, the scars that crisscrossed over his chest, pink and discolored, pulling and tight, were nothing.

Just like she didn't have the legs of a normal woman, he didn't have the chest of a normal man.

All the bones were there, but the muscle and fat that might have laid under, the smooth skin, even the hair, none of it was there.

"I'm sorry. You have that because I'm alive. It almost makes me wish you hadn't gone back in."

That hadn't been what he had meant at all.

He did not tell her that though. That wasn't what he was trying to say. Although, honestly he wasn't sure he could tell her what he was trying to say.

"I'd do it again in a heartbeat. Again and again." It was true. The pain he'd suffered, the teasing, and the bitterness and anger, it was all worth it. Just because Eliza stood before him, breathing and alive.

Sure she had scars, but she was alive.

"Hines?" Eliza said. His name coming from her sounded... He wasn't even sure. It did something to his chest. Made him feel bigger somehow.

"What?" he murmured.

"You saved my life. I owe you...everything," she said, shaking her head and looking around like the words that she was trying to say would somehow come out of the woodwork. "How could you think that I would...just think you were a story?"

She looked back at him, her eyes piercing. He almost took a step back. "How could you think that I would sell this, what you did, and just be here to get a scoop? How could you? I don't understand."

"It could have been anyone who went back for you. It didn't have to be me. Anyone standing there, anyone who would have heard you, would have gone."

"But no one else heard."

His fingers clenched around his T-shirt. His throat tightened. She was right. Even though there had been five or six other people around, he was the only one who had heard her. He was the only one who had gone back, and he had gone despite the fact that the people who were standing with him had begged him not to go. They'd told him that he was just hearing things, that he was making up the voice in his head, that his brain was trying to trick him into getting glory that wasn't there.

He didn't know what glory there was in dying, but he had ignored them and gone anyway.

"I've seen the worst of people. There are plenty of people who would do pretty much anything for money, not even as much money as you would get for selling my story. Please don't act like it's crazy that I think that that might have been what you were here for."

"But you've been with me for two weeks. You know me. Maybe not all of me, but you see me. Do I seem like the kind of person who would do that?"

"You don't, but how do I know? How do I know it's not just an act? People keep up masks for years. You could do it for a couple of weeks."

"Are you ever going to believe me?"

"Why do you want to know? What do you want from me?"

Did she just want him to let his guard down? Was this like Samson and Delilah where Delilah nagged Samson until he couldn't stand it anymore and gave her whatever she wanted?

He always felt bad for Samson. He had loved Delilah. And Delilah betrayed him. He wanted to be able to trust her. Wanted to be able to give her the secrets to his soul and have them be safe with her. Isn't that what every human wanted? To have a soulmate who held their secrets safe. Who stood beside them and loved them no matter what their scars looked like inside and out.

He wasn't any different.

But he didn't want to trust. He'd done that, and he'd been burned. Literally. He didn't think he would be able to hold himself together if he gave someone the keys to his heart, and she turned around and sold them.

How could he explain to her? How could he get her to see?

"I just want you to trust me," she said, and it was obvious she didn't have any clue of the fight that was going on inside of him.

"It's taken me a long time to build what I have here. To leave my old life and create something here. I don't want someone coming and unearthing everything about me, and then selling it to the highest bidder. That would be a betrayal I'm not sure I could forgive."

"Does it matter? Are secrets really that important? Why do we care whether people know or not? You're not hiding anything embarrassing or wrong. What you did was brave and amazing. But it sounds like I'm trying to talk you into telling me things, and I'm not. Not because I want to write about them. Just because I want to know you. But..." She smiled a little. "We talked a couple weeks ago about just showing up in your life, without expectations. And then making the most of it. I think part of that is not having expectations for other people. I can't expect you to want to share with me things that you want to keep to yourself. I'm sorry I pried."

She looked at the wheelchair. "Today you get to go out. Let's not ruin it by talking about this anymore."

"I—"

She put a hand up. "No. We can make this a great day." She took a deep breath. "Let me get you some coffee first. I must've beaten Miller here, since you don't have a mug sitting beside you."

"He was here pretty late last night. I told him not to worry about coming in first thing. He said he didn't have any fields to spray and maybe he would sleep in a little."

"Well, that's exciting. For me. I've been looking forward to this."

"You have no idea," he said as she walked around him into the kitchen.

The way she moved around was different than listening to Miller. He could almost hear her gracefulness, and Miller didn't hum to himself.

It was a hymn. One he would recognize anywhere. "Amazing Grace." He almost started humming with her. For not being a morning person, she certainly came in in a good mood every single morning. He couldn't remember a morning in the last two weeks that she hadn't been, if not cheerful, at least happy.

"You seem to be doing pretty good with your morning person transformation," he said as she brought a steaming mug of coffee out to him.

"Thanks. It's still a little bit of a struggle to get out of bed, and I don't wake up without the alarm, but I'm pleased."

"There aren't a lot of people who do wake up without an alarm."

"You do."

"Maybe I set my phone."

"You're awake every morning when I come, and I'm pretty sure you don't set the alarm on your phone."

"You're right. There's just something about the sunrise that calls to me. I wake up every day, eager to see it. That's what gets me out of bed, yeah."

She sipped her coffee for a little bit, looking out the window at the sky that was just barely starting to lighten.

He loved this time of morning. Loved the calm peacefulness. And he appreciated that she seemed to respect it. That there was an awe about the morning with her as well.

Finally, when his coffee was half drunk, he said, "I'm going to use the restroom, then, if it isn't too cold," he eyed her skirt, "I'm ready to go."

"It was cold but not freezing. Sweatshirt weather. I had a beanie cap on too."

"You left it in the car?"

She lifted her shoulder, looking abashed. "I do have a little bit of vanity."

"Maybe you need to go out and get it. I don't want you to get cold."

"I hardly think I'll get cold. It's pretty exciting that you're finally able to get up and about. This was really kind of Miller and Gideon."

"I couldn't agree more."

She came over and set her coffee down beside his, leaning into him and giving him a hand up.

By now, they had a familiar routine to get him up out of his chair.

They did it together, and it almost felt natural. As natural as taking her hand and strolling in the moonlight.

Of course, he had never done that, but the idea, once it was in his head, was a good one. He liked it. Maybe he'd have that opportunity.

And maybe he was getting way too excited about something that was never going to happen. When Eliza was around, he forgot he was scarred and ugly. She made him feel, if not handsome, intelligent and fun. Like he was worth coming to see.

But he was just an obligation to her. He always forgot.

By the time he was done using the restroom and had come back and drunk the rest of his coffee, he had gotten his thinking straightened out again.

He settled into the wheelchair, frustrated that he wouldn't be able to move it himself. But thankful that his broken bones might twinge, but they didn't hurt anymore.

"I think I'm going to have to go out the door backward. In order to open it. Then, I think we'll have to turn around in order to shut it."

"We'll get it figured out. I might be able to shut it with my foot. But I'm not sure I want to go down the ramp backward. Not my first time anyway."

"Well, as long as you are wheels down, backward or frontward should both give us the same result."

"That's true. I suppose though, if we're going to have a wreck, I'd rather wreck feetfirst than headfirst."

"All right. I've heard you, and I'll do what you say. We'll go down feetfirst." She maneuvered the chair out around so they backed through the door, and he was able to shut it with his foot by stretching it out. He felt the pull in his leg, but it wasn't a terrible pain, and the doctor had said in their video chat appointment two days ago that he could begin to move around a little. As long as he didn't put any weight on it. That was a complete and absolute no-no for several weeks, and the doctor had been sure that he understood it.

True to her word, she turned him around and they went down the ramp together.

"We can tell Miller when he gets here that it works really well."

"Is that relief in your voice?" He was only half teasing her, because she did sound relieved.

"You don't understand the pressure. If I would have wrecked you in your wheelchair, can you imagine the flak I would take for that?"

"From Miller and Gideon, whom you barely see. No one else knows."

"I told my aunt this morning. Although, she's not going to give me any flak for it. Not much anyway."

"Does she know that I'm the one…" He let his words trail off, because it seemed kind of like tooting his own horn to say he was the one who saved her.

"She does. She knew that was why I came to Sweet Water."

"Really?" he asked.

"Yeah. I had heard that you were around here somewhere. For years, when I had some vacation or some time off, I would come, visit my aunt, and look around for you. There were rumors of a recluse, but no one was willing to tell an outsider where you lived. And my aunt didn't know, even though it doesn't seem like there's too much stuff that happens in Sweet Water that she doesn't know about."

"Interesting. I didn't know it wasn't common knowledge."

"When Miller came, I think that's when people started hearing about it more. Just because you guys are friends and he would pick some things up for you."

"That makes sense." He knew he could count on Miller to be completely discreet, but he probably had said that he was picking some things up for a friend, and people had put two and two together.

"She talked to me about you this morning," Eliza said thoughtfully as she pushed his wheelchair in the direction of the barn.

"She did?" he asked, surprised again. Of course, he could have said the same thing to Eliza two weeks ago—that Miller had warned him about her.

"I think so. I... I'm not sure why."

"Maybe because you spent every waking second at my house for the last two weeks. Maybe she wants you to have time off."

"She told me that if I wanted some time off, she would come and sit with you while I did some errands in town. But I don't really feel like I need it."

He didn't say anything right away, because he wasn't sure how he felt about Eliza's aunt coming to his house.

But he was even less sure about how he felt about Eliza's aunt warning her about him. It was true that he hadn't had a very good family growing up. The only stable thing about it was that his sister consistently moved with him. They had been blessed to not be separated.

"How is your sister doing?" Eliza said, maybe to try to change the subject.

"I haven't talked to her since shortly after the accident. She doesn't know where I am."

"She doesn't?"

"She probably knows I'm in North Dakota. I don't know. I haven't talked to her."

"Why not?" Eliza asked, sounding shocked. "I'm sorry. Maybe I'm prying. I don't want you to feel like you have to tell me, if that's information you'd rather keep to yourself."

"After the accident, I was out walking with her. Well, I had a cane and I was limping. You know how grotesque I look. It was even worse back then, because it was before a lot of my plastic surgeries. People made fun of me, and she ended up in tears. I knew that being with me would embarrass her, make her life harder. It had already been hard enough, and I didn't want that for her, so I decided at that point, after my surgeries to repair my face, I would be leaving."

"And that's what you did."

"I didn't finish the surgeries. They didn't seem like they were doing that much anyway, and I was ready to leave. It's hard whenever you go out somewhere, people stare at you, like you're some kind of monster."

"I suppose that people don't mean to, it's just... Sometimes when you see something that's unusual, you have a tendency to look at it to try to figure it out."

"I didn't want to be something people try to figure out."

She continued as though he hadn't interrupted. "But people get used to what they see, and then they don't need to look at it anymore. It just comes naturally."

He waited. Sure enough, she added a little bit.

"That's what happened with me. When I talk to you now, I don't think about your scars, the way you look. I think about your character and your sense of humor. How you're smart and funny and I enjoy being with you. Scars don't really register. That would happen with everyone, but you just need to give them a little bit of time."

He didn't say anything. He supposed that was the way it was with his horses too. They just needed time to get used to things. Not necessarily his scars, but him in general.

"This is the horse I was looking at the day the accident happened, when I broke my arm and leg," he murmured as she pushed his chair to the corral where a beautiful blue roan mare stared at them from the other side.

Beautiful in his eyes, since she still was mostly skin and bones. Maybe it was his imagination, but it seemed like she had put weight on, even though the last time he'd seen her he'd barely been able to make her out in the shadows of the stall.

Little by little, bit by bit, every day she got a bit better. That was true in nature, true with his horses, and true for himself.

His future was in his hands.

# Chapter 10

Ellen opened the oven door and pulled out the brownie cheesecake she'd made for that evening's dessert.

Her new cousin had been born just a few days ago and Uncle Tadgh was bringing Aunt Ashley and the new little one home from the hospital. They'd be there in just an hour and she wanted to have the perfect meal ready for them.

Beaver, her Australian Shepherd pup, whined at her feet.

"It's okay, Beaver," she said before there was a short rap on the door. It opened before she could call out and the neighbor boys Roger and Edgar, Travis's brothers, walked in.

"We've been following the scent of fresh brownies for the last fifteen minutes. Led us right to your house," Roger said with a grin.

"These are for supper," Ellen said. She waited while the boys' faces fell in disappointment. "But I made these earlier as a test run and you guys can have the whole pan. There's only one piece missing where Charlie and Charlene tried it out."

Big, happy smiles lit up their faces again. They were high school age, but still sweet, and food made them happy.

"Can we take anything we don't eat home with us?" Edgar asked.

"You sure can," Ellen replied, knowing her aunt and uncle cared for Edgar and Roger as much as they had cared for their older brother, Travis.

"Have you heard from Travis lately?" she asked as she grabbed plates and set them at the table where the boys had already seated themselves.

"Sure did. He was home for a visit last week. We offered to walk over with him to see you, but he didn't seem interested," Roger's gaze followed the cheesecake brownie pan as Ellen set it on the table so he wouldn't have noticed how his words made Ellen's whole face feel like a weather-beaten barn board.

Travis had been home and hadn't come to see her?

His letters had been getting fewer and fewer, but she still wrote weekly anyway, figuring he was busy.

But he'd been home. He'd had time to travel the whole way from Chicago to North Dakota and hadn't taken the time to come see her?

"Hey! What's this white stuff?" Edgar asked with his mouth full. Apparently not knowing what it was hadn't kept him from eating it.

His words barely registered as Ellen still tried to figure out why Travis wouldn't have at least stopped in to say hi. He could have come with his brothers and grabbed some food like he'd done the whole time he'd been in junior high and high school.

"It's a brownie cheesecake. The white stuff is cheesecake," Ellen said, her words sounding faint.

"Oh. It's pretty good," Edgar said, his mouth full again.

"Trav said he had a party to go to. Some chick he knew that coached the cheer squad or something," Roger said, and at least he waited until his mouth was empty before he spoke.

Shanna. Travis had found time to go to one of Shanna's parties, but hadn't made time to come see her.

That cut hard.

She swallowed, but her mouth was dry and it felt like there was a pin cushion lodged there anyway.

"We told him you'd have food, but he musta had something he wanted more." Roger smirked and poked his brother with his elbow.

Ellen pulled air into her lungs and tried to shut her brain down. He'd said he wanted to be friends, nothing more.

Although he'd also said he was going to be working hard and wouldn't have much time. That was what he'd told her when he'd not written for two weeks the last time. She'd believed him and had told him that she'd keep writing, since she figured she'd never be too busy to give a little of her time to Travis.

But he'd blown her off and went to see Shanna instead.

The boys didn't linger at the table and it wasn't long, although it felt like forever, before they left, cheesecake brownies tucked under their arm.

Ellen barely waited for the door to close before she sank down on the floor next to Beaver, putting her arm around her dog and burying her head in his neck, her tears seeping into his fur.

Angry tears.

No, the anger just masked the hurt she felt.

Well, it served her right. Travis had said he wanted to just be friends and she'd agreed. So, if she was upset, she only had herself to blame. After all, she wouldn't be hurt if Roger or Edger went to someone's party rather than visited with her.

Although, Travis had said he wanted to kiss her. There was that.

But he must have changed his mind. And he'd never said he felt anything toward her, so maybe she'd misunderstood about the kiss.

Still, she was done writing to him. If he wanted to hang out with Shanna, he could get Shanna to write. If Shanna could spell enough words correctly to put a letter together.

That wasn't nice. And she wanted to be better than that. Saying a small prayer of apology and asking God to help her actually be the person her mind knew she should be, she lifted her chin.

Just because Travis had snubbed her, ditched her, not made time for her, that didn't mean that she would return his actions in kind. No. She would continue to write like she had promised. She would keep her word and she would be the best friend she could be, even if he was unkind or inconsiderate. *That* was the kind of person she wanted to be.

Later that evening after the baby had come home and Ellen had spent several hours holding her so Aunt Ashley could sleep a bit, Ellen sat at the small desk in her room with her pencil poised over a blank piece of paper.

She was going to be a good friend, but friends could admit to friends when they'd been hurt, right? She wasn't sure.

Bending her head, she started to write.

---

*Dear Travis,*

*My new cousin came home today. I haven't seen Uncle Tadgh look so pleased since you walked across that stage at school and accepted your diploma.*

*Aunt Ashley looked exhausted. So, even though I've never held a baby before, they let me keep her while Uncle Tadgh took Aunt Ashley into their bedroom and made her take a nap.*

*I was a little nervous at first, but all she did was sleep. She smelled so good. Like a crisp winter morning when the sun is just coming up over the horizon and the air is clean and pure and fresh snow is lying on the ground like a snug blanket. I know you know what I'm talking about.*

*That's not quite the way a new baby smells, but it's close. I could breathe that smell forever.*

*I've been working on teaching Beaver some easy commands. He's smart and learns fast, but his attention span is about two seconds long. I've had to develop more patience than I ever thought I'd need in order to keep from getting upset when he forgets that we're working and wants to play. He's like a little kid. Like you used to be.*

*Actually, you were never like a little kid. You had to grow up too fast. He's like your brothers. You protected them and they had a lot more of a childhood than you did.*

---

*School is going good, but I have a feeling it's going to be hard to leave the new baby and sit in class all day. It's worse than leaving a newborn calf, that's for sure. Maybe I can talk Uncle Tadgh into homeschooling me. Aunt Ashley might be on my side if I promise to watch the baby six hours every day.*

*So...I know you haven't written in three weeks, and that is okay if you're working.*

*But Roger and Edgar were here today and...they said you were home. It made me sad and hurt my feelings that you were home and didn't come see me. I thought we were friends?*

*They also said that you went to someone's party and I assume that was Shanna. That hurt, too, but I guess it shouldn't have. Just I thought you were better friends with me than you were with Shanna, but if you have time to see her and not see me, maybe I'm wrong.*

*Do you want me to keep writing to you?*

*Your friend,*

*Ellen*

# Chapter 11

The horse in front of them was pathetically skinny. Eliza couldn't believe it was even still alive. How did something that was basically a skeleton even survive?

But as they stood there watching her, the sunrise slowly brightening the eastern sky, the horse snorted, pawed the ground, and shook her head.

She might look like she was half dead, but she still had spirit.

"She has sass," she said, not necessarily to Hines, but she was just talking to herself.

"No. She's a fighter. That's part of what drew me to her. She... She's had a pretty rough time."

"Yeah, I don't know what her story is, but you can tell she struggled."

She could see how he would relate to a horse like that. Of course, he never lost so much weight, but he'd gone through some really difficult things. She could see how that would have given him patience to deal with horses like this.

"Do all of your horses look like this when they come?" she asked.

"No. Some of them are mangy and dirty, and some of them look just fine, people just don't want them anymore because of behavioral problems. Sometimes it's not easy to try to figure out what it's going to take in order to fix the problem."

"Are you always able to fix it?"

"No. Sometimes we just have to learn to live with it." He shrugged a little. "Sometimes we can shave the rough edges off, and you don't have a perfect horse—no horse is perfect—but you have something that people can ride and enjoy."

"Every horse?"

"So far. I'm not saying that there's not going to be a horse someday that I can't find a way to fix, but so far, not."

"I bet it takes a lot of time."

"Yeah. It's going to take even longer with this one because of my issues, but they can take a year or even more."

"And a lot of patience."

"Yeah. Sometimes it takes a really long time to see a break-through. You want to give up."

"But you don't."

"No."

She couldn't help but think that that was the way life was in so many ways. Sometimes it felt like things were never going to get better. That there was no point in trying, but if a person just kept working and working at it, things almost had to work out.

She supposed Hines was probably thinking the exact same thing. Especially after what they'd talked about earlier inside. Where she showed him her scars. And he'd shown her his.

There were times lying in the hospital room where she thought she would never have a life again. Never have a day where she didn't have pain. Never have hope.

But she hadn't given up.

Obviously he hadn't either. He had to have had the same thoughts at times.

Now, after they'd healed, their lives had gone in different direc-tions. But she could understand why he would have wanted to close himself off. If her scars were that obvious, she couldn't say that she wouldn't have wanted to do the same thing.

"If I hadn't come here, I wouldn't have learned I was good with horses, and I wouldn't have been able to spend so much time doing something I love. I... I probably didn't need to be so reclusive, but beyond that, I can't say that I regret it."

"I think you have a good thing going. The only thing I regret in talking to you is that you're not talking to your sister. Just because something happened to you doesn't mean she loves you less."

She remembered them as being very close.

"That's water under the bridge."

"You guys survived a lot of foster care together. You seemed really close growing up. And I wasn't even your age."

"We were. She was just two years younger than me, and she was the one thing that I felt like I could protect. And the state was really good at trying to keep us together. I can't say that they always did everything perfectly, but I do appreciate that about them."

"Aren't you curious as to what's become of her?"

"I just know she's better off without me."

"Did you let her make that decision?"

"I didn't have to." There was irritation in his voice, and he used his one hand to try to move the wheelchair forward. It turned and didn't roll forward. She almost didn't touch the handles, letting him do what he would by himself, but that wasn't being a very good caretaker. So, she swallowed her irritation at him, put her hand on the handle, and helped to go forward.

He talked softly to the horse as she pricked her ears up at him, although she did not come closer.

"I've had Miller feeding her hay and water. After a few days, I had him start adding grain to her feeding. So she gets as much hay as she wants and a little bit of grain every day. We've been increasing it slowly. Horses can get sick if you change their diet too fast, and she's already been through enough."

"Did you have the vet come look at her?"

"Lark came right after the horse did. You were there when Lark was in the house talking about the horse."

"I remember. I was making supper. But I didn't realize Lark was the vet. She seemed like such a sweet young girl."

"She's thirty-five. At least."

"Goodness. She doesn't look that old."

"Life goes on, but I'm almost positive she's that old. Maybe even older." He paused for a moment, then he added, "She never married. There are always rumors that go around any small town, but it sounds like her story is rather tragic."

"Her boyfriend died?"

"I think he jilted her. I think he loved her, and she loved him, but there was something that wouldn't let them get together, and then he married someone else."

"I might have to ask around about that. I hadn't heard."

"You're going to write a story about him?" There wasn't as much teasing in his voice as he wanted there to be as he turned around to look at her. He still didn't completely trust her. Obviously.

"No. I'm just curious. Sounds romantic. Or tragic like you said."

"I guess I was talking about her to get the subject off me, but I don't want to throw Lark under the bus. She's a nice lady, and she's great with my horses."

"She sounded very concerned, but I guess I just didn't think she looked like a vet. I don't know. I didn't realize."

"She has a girls' home too. She and her associate, Mabel."

"She's a vet, and she runs a girls' home?"

Had she ever heard of such a thing?

"It's an unofficial thing. They just have girls show up, they take them under their wings and care for them. They put them to work on the farm, and often a girl who struggled just needed someone to take an interest in her and give her something to do."

She wanted to ask more about Lark, but Miller pulled in just then.

He shut his lights off, and the pickup door slammed as he got out.

The sunrise had brightened the sky into a brilliant orange, with pinks and blues edging the color as the sky gradually lightened.

It was a glorious display, and Miller came over and stood beside them without saying anything, the three of them watching the sky change, as darkness turned to day.

"Glad I didn't sleep in any longer," Miller finally said, indicating that he was happy he hadn't missed the sunrise.

"It's not every day you get a show like that."

"It always reminds me that God loves me. Every morning, He wakes up and tells me with the sunrise. Sometimes I'm awake to see it, sometimes I miss His message."

Eliza bit her lips. She'd never heard someone explain it quite like that, but if she hadn't been trying to be a morning person before, that inspired her to try even harder. After all, if God had a message for her first thing in the morning, she didn't want to miss it.

"I'm glad Eliza's here with you. I'm going to need to go on a trip overnight. We have some late-season spraying to do down in Colorado, and unless you want to bring someone else to do the horses, she's going to have to take care of them."

"I haven't thought about it. I..."

"I can do it," Eliza said immediately.

"Are you sure?" Hines asked, looking back at her.

"I am. I mean, as long as it's within my skill set. Do I have to cut the hay and bale it before I feed it?" she asked, being a little facetious.

"Nothing that complicated. But you just want to have an eye on the horses, not be scared of them."

"Are they going to hurt me?"

"Sometimes they bite," Hines said easily as Miller snorted.

"Sometimes?"

"You just have to watch. Here, I'll show you. Not with this horse," he said as he indicated the direction he wanted to go.

"We really need to think of a name for that horse," Eliza said as she pushed him beside Miller.

"I think you named her this morning," Hines said easily.

"What?" she asked, trying to think back if she had called the horse by name. She didn't think she had.

"You said she had sass. I thought Sassy was the perfect name."

"Oh. Maybe it is." But... She looked back over her shoulder at the horse who was watching them leave. Her eyes had been on them the whole time they'd been there. "I actually do think it fits."

"I thought it did too. I thought it was a really good name. Glad you thought of it."

She laughed, because they both knew she hadn't named her on purpose.

They talked together as they walked through the barn, with the men bantering back and forth, giving instructions to her, which she knew she would never remember. But as long as Hines went out with her, she didn't see them doing anything that she thought she couldn't imitate. And if Hines had another week to heal, who knew what he would be able to do by then.

They went back in, with Miller leaving and Hines and her spending another day together in the same way that they'd grown accustomed to. Only, that night before she left, Hines told her that if she'd just give him another week, he would be fine if she had her aunt come to stay while she went and had a day off.

She did need an entire day off, and she did want to talk to Kenni and ask a few questions around town. So, she told him she would happily work another week, and then her Aunt April would be in to see him.

# Chapter 12

"And that's all I know about Lark." Kenni shrugged her shoulders and then put the last bite of her sandwich in her mouth.

Eliza looked down at her half-eaten food.

She'd been so busy listening to Kenni tell her about Lark that she forgot to eat.

Kenni hadn't really told her anything that Hines hadn't already said. Other than Lark had nine brothers and sisters, and the Stryker family was a pillar of the Sweet Water community.

"It'd be nice to see her find someone," she murmured, her mind whirling. Maybe the matchmaking steer that had been hanging out at their house could go find Lark.

"I don't think she wants anyone. The man she loved got married, and she just wasn't interested in anyone else. So she's devoted her life to animals and to the girls that come into her place. I can't fault her." Kenni lifted her shoulder again.

They'd been eating at the diner, and the diner had gone from quite busy to almost completely empty.

"I appreciate you telling me about Lark." Eliza tried to get her mind off the woman she barely knew and to think about her new friend. "How's married life treating you?" she asked as she picked up her sandwich. There was no point in her not finishing what was one of the most delicious sandwiches she'd ever eaten, just because Lark had a tragic love story.

"It's going well. I've settled into the farm and found most of my jobs to be fun. In fact, I've been having so much fun with my pig, Scrunchy."

"Scrunchy?"

"Her mom's name is Munchy." Kenni shook her head. "I know. I can't even believe it myself."

Eliza pressed her mouth closed. Kenni had been a princess for a long time, with the paparazzi following her every move. Now, she was sitting in a diner, talking with her mouth full, and bragging about her pet pig.

"I had to bottle-feed her for a while, because she was away from her mom. The steer we were talking about, Billy, brought her to my house."

"I think I remember seeing her there."

"So since I was bottle-feeding her, I wanted to find a baby stroller, and that's a good thing. I mean, I carried her around everywhere I went. Because she had to be kept warm. Anyway, my husband put his foot down over that, or you would be sitting here talking to me with my pig in a baby carriage beside us."

Kenni's voice held all the humor in the world and none of the snobbery that a person might have thought that someone who used to be a princess might have held.

Eliza had found her very down to earth and quite a nice friend. In fact, she couldn't imagine having a better friend. She had accepted Eliza right away, despite the fact that Eliza had arrived with the paparazzi.

Unlike Hines, who still didn't quite trust her.

She wasn't sure that their discussion a week ago had done anything to help. Nor the fact that she had worn a skirt so that he could see her legs.

Maybe she should have just kept them covered.

"Oh my goodness, here come the girls," Kenni said, looking like the girls were the most adorable things ever.

"The girls?" Eliza asked.

"Tell me you haven't heard about how Merritt and Sorrell, Jane's daughters, matched up their mom using the Marry Me Chicken?"

"I think you might have told me that story a while ago, but maybe I didn't realize that they were her daughters."

"Yes. And the tall one, Toni, has been trying to get her mom matched up as well. But I'm afraid that her efforts have not been going as well."

"Her mom is still single?"

"As far as I know," Kenni said before she waved her hand and said, "Hi, girls! How are you doing?"

The girls smiled and then changed their direction, coming over to the table.

Eliza supposed growing up in a diner had taught Merritt and Sorrell that they could talk to anyone.

"How's Scrunchy?" the tall girl asked.

"I was just telling my friend Eliza about her, saying how much she was growing." Kenni turned to Eliza. "This is Toni, and Sorrell and Merritt are Jane's daughters."

"Nice to meet you all," Eliza said, trying to put their names in her memory. She wasn't always very good at remembering people's names, but she knew it was something that was important. She tried to make the effort.

"What are you guys doing this evening? Do you have school-work?" she asked. School was always a safe topic for kids of that age when she didn't know what else to say to them.

"We set a date up with my mom." Toni looked around before she lowered her voice. "We made Marry Me Chicken, and we have her eating it at my place with the new man in town."

"We have to act fast, because when men come into town, other people snatch them up right away," Sorrell said.

Her sister added, "We weren't sure about this one, but we figured we better do something fast, before someone else grabbed him."

"You mean, you weren't sure about him how?" Eliza asked.

"Whether or not he would make a good dad. That's the whole point. Toni needs a dad just like we did," Sorrell said.

Eliza nodded sagely, although inside she was smiling. She wondered how their mom felt about this. She could only imagine. She wondered even more when Toni added, "Mom didn't know what I was doing, so she was really surprised when we announced that she was going to be eating by herself with Dallas. That's his name."

Eliza grinned. What she wouldn't do to be a fly on the wall at that house tonight.

# Chapter 13

Mallie sat with her head in her hand, trying not to look as bored as she felt.

It was hard.

"And after I get the spreadsheets figured out, then I have to make sure that the data is entered into the proper areas in each compartment. I'm sure you can understand how difficult that is, and completely time-consuming. Not anyone can do work like that. I'm told that I'm the best in the business. Then, after a hard workday, I like to go home and unwind. The first thing I do is take my shoes off, because who can stand to be in shoes all day, right?" Dallas laughed, and Mallie had the feeling that she was supposed to laugh along with him. "And then I escape into a fantasy world. Picture Mr. Rogers, only modern day."

Mallie didn't have any trouble picturing Mr. Rogers and Dallas, only she had a feeling that Mr. Rogers's pretend neighborhood was much more interesting than Dallas's, whatever his fantasy world was.

"Still, I can't say that I don't love my job. It definitely has perks. I, for example, get five weeks of paid vacation every year. Actually, next year I get bumped up to six. That's a good bit of vacation, and my health insurance benefits are out-of-this-world good. I definitely have a lot to bring to the table in a marriage. I've been told I'm quite the eligible bachelor since my last divorce."

"Last divorce?" Mallie asked, thinking that it sounded like he had at least two under his belt.

"Yeah. I've lived with several women, and that never worked out either. I can bring you up to speed on my dating history. There is quite a lot of it. I have quite the extensive experience, and have actually counseled a lot of my friends in the dating world. They appreciate my advice, just because of my extensive experience. I definitely say do not move in together after the first date. You need to have at least three dates under your belt before you move in together. Now, you can sleep together, of course, but you've got to make sure that if you invite her to your house, she goes home. Actually, I always say that after the first date, we should sleep together at the woman's house. So, just letting you know my policy up front, so when we continue our date, you know the score. I suppose, it depends on how good the good-night kiss is, and let me tell you, I've got quite extensive experience in that area as well. I can let you know, within the first five seconds of the kiss, whether the woman and I click or not. I've got it down to that good of a science."

"Well," Mallie said, wishing she hadn't eaten the three bites of chicken that she had. She felt like they were going to come back up.

"I know. Quite impressive. My friends all are amazed at how easily I can read someone by how they kiss. People always appreciate my extensive expertise. Not only am I quite skilled at reading people, but I'm quite skilled at kissing as well."

"Interesting," Mallie said, telling herself she couldn't look at her watch. It had been only about two or three minutes since the last time.

"Of course, when a woman moves in with me, she needs to share the kitchen with my mother. My mother also always gets the master bedroom anywhere we live. So, whatever woman I'm with needs to accept that. And my mother does not do dishes, so when a woman moves in with me, she needs to understand that my mother will cook, but she will not do dishes."

"I see. Important."

"That's right. I like to keep my mother happy. It makes life easier for everyone." Dallas gave a small smile. "Of course you know what I mean."

She had no idea what he meant, but she wasn't going to ask because she didn't want to spend the next fifteen minutes talking about Dallas's mother. As nice as the woman probably was.

"Actually, I'm not sure what is in this chicken, but it's quite delicious. Are you going to eat the rest of what's on your plate?" He nodded to the plate of chicken that she had.

Toni and her friends had dished their plates and then snuck out. She had no idea that they had invited someone they had apparently met yesterday to eat supper at their house, and she had even less idea that Toni was going to spend the evening with Sorrell and Merritt, planned of course.

She was going to have a lot to say to Toni when Toni got home.

"No. I wasn't."

"Do you mind if I eat that? Man, that is good. Of course, the onions might make my breath smell a little bit strong for our good-night kiss, or possibly the prelude for more, depending on how skillful I am this evening, and I'm feeling quite skillful," Dallas snickered, like that was funny, "but skill can overcome a multitude of issues, even onion breath," he said as he reached over and took Mallie's plate from her, setting it on top of his own and digging in.

Mallie didn't bother to tell him that he was using her fork.

She didn't usually get quite so close and personal with people that she just met, and it was fine with her if he did, as long as he didn't expect her to be like him.

"Did you say you have the recipe for this?" he asked, his mouth full. Which, she really didn't mind people talking with their mouth full, she just minded whenever they spit food out while they spoke.

She wiped her nose off. "No. I don't. My daughter does, and I'm sure you can talk to her about it when she gets home, which, if you'll excuse me for a moment, I probably ought to text her and ask her where she is."

"No. Go right ahead. I admire a woman who can keep track of her children. That was the problem that I had with Sally, who lived with me for seven months. Her kids were always everywhere. They were so annoying. They did their homework at the kitchen table even though they had desks in the room. Then they always had to eat before bed. They looked at me like they expected me to make them popcorn or something. It was just way too much. I was not ready to be a father, just couldn't handle all of the pressure of having people at my table, making popcorn at night. It was just way, way too much. I was going to ask her to leave, but she did me a favor and went ahead and moved before I could. She wasn't that good in bed anyway."

Mallie stopped listening and pulled up the texting app on her phone.

**Toni, you need to get back home right now. I cannot believe you left me alone with this man.**

She looked up and smiled a little, but Dallas hadn't even noticed that she looked away, he was still droning on about how exceptionally skillful he was at... Mallie's eyes widened. Apparently he'd dated a gymnast. Ugh. The chicken lurched in her stomach.

Her phone buzzed, and she looked down.

**Why? Do you like him?**

She was so tempted to unload on Toni, to tell her that he lived with his mother, which wouldn't be bad, except it felt a little odd that his mother was apparently placed before his wife in the pecking order of the home. Mallie was perfectly okay if he found someone who was okay with that situation, but that someone was not going to be her.

**No. I need to get to bed. I have to work tomorrow.**

She couldn't believe that that was all she was going to say, but she knew that Toni would rescue her. And she needed to be rescued.

She wasn't sure how much longer she could stand to sit and listen to this man. She didn't want to be rude. So, as he finished his chicken, putting the last bite in his mouth, she said, "So, I have to work tomorrow, and I need to get to bed. I would invite you to stay, but I really can't."

That was true, and she didn't want to hurt his feelings, but if he didn't leave, she was going to have to get more firm.

"I thought there was dessert?"

"No. I don't think there's any dessert. I'm sorry."

The girls might have said something about a cake in the kitchen, but she wasn't going to go look for it. And she sure wasn't going to serve it. She heard enough about the women Dallas had dated and slept with. And his skills in both areas.

She needed to get him out.

# Chapter 14

"**I** know you mean well, Toni, but you can't do this again."

Toni stood in front of her mother with her head hanging down.

Her mom hadn't yelled at her, exactly, but when Toni came home and her mom was escorting her dinner date out the door, explaining that yes, it was only 6:30, but she went to bed early, as she had a big workday in the morning, Toni figured she was probably going to be in trouble.

This was only the second time she'd taken a gamble on the Marry Me Chicken. The other time, she'd accidentally chosen someone who was just out of high school.

She hadn't known. He had a full beard, and with a cowboy hat on, he looked like he was her mom's age.

That date hadn't lasted past the first course either. Her mom had practically run out of the apartment scared to death that she was going to get slapped with some kind of sexual abuse of a minor or something.

Toni hadn't had the nerve to try again until now.

Dallas had seemed like a nice person. He was serious and boring, the kind of man her mama claimed she wanted. Someone who was going to be responsible and not just dump them whenever things got difficult.

"I'm sorry, Mom," Toni said, feeling hopeless.

"Oh, Toni," her mom said, taking a step toward her and putting her arms around her.

Toni loved the way her mother smelled. She wanted to bury her nose in her mom's shirt like she did when she was little and just let all the cares of the world fade away.

"Why do you do this, Toni?" her mom asked gently, not loosening the tight hold she had with her arms around her.

"I just want a dad. Everybody else has one, and Sorrell and Merritt found a really great one. I want one too."

"Did you ever think that maybe you just need to be happy with your life the way it is? Maybe, instead of thinking about the things that you want and don't have, you can be grateful for the things that you do?"

"I know. I just... I just want a dad who will love you, and love me, and make us a family."

"And aren't you and I a family? Aren't we happy together?"

"We are."

"Now, are we? Is there something that you need that you're not telling me?" Her mom loosened her grip, put two hands on her shoulders, and pushed her back. "Toni?" she asked, her brows raised.

Toni shook her head. There really wasn't anything she wanted. Her mom had made sure that they got everything she needed. It was just... "Don't you want a husband? Don't you want romance?"

Her mom sighed, a deep sigh, and then she put her arm around Toni's shoulders and led her to the couch where they both sank down into the cushions. Her mom leaned back, and Toni snuggled up against her side.

Her mom sat quietly for a few minutes as though she were thinking about what she wanted to say.

Finally she started to talk.

"I do. I think, I could be wrong, but I think most women want romance. But sometimes I think what we long for is just a substitute for what God wants to give us. We look to other people to fulfill the emotional needs we have and don't pay attention to what God wants to do for us."

"But you can't see God. You can't hear Him. You can't hug Him."

"I know. And I don't mean to belittle the place that people have in our lives. We need people to validate us. We need people to hug us. We need people to listen to us. I'm not saying we don't. But I'm saying sometimes what we have a tendency to do is to always be looking for a human solution to the problem that God wants to solve. We just don't give Him the opportunity."

"That's God giving you a husband again?"

"It's a little bit like that, yeah. You asked me if I wanted romance. I do. I think we all do. But I don't want to make romance my idol."

"Like build an altar and worship it here in the living room?" Toni asked, even though she knew that wasn't what her mom meant. It just seemed weird to say that romance could become an idol.

"Of course not. Just sometimes we build up in our head these things that we need, and we don't really need them. What we need is God. We go chasing after this thing or that thing thinking that it's going to satisfy us, and it never does. We'd be better off opening up our Bible, even though for some reason we really don't want to, and seeing what God has to say to us. He wants to be our friend, He wants to listen to us, He wants us to talk to Him. He wants to be everything to us. And so often, we put other things ahead of Him, not that we build an altar and sit and worship at them physically, but in our hearts and our minds, those are the things we long for. Whether it's romance, or whether it's recreation, some people long for their vacation, or they can't wait to go play golf, or go shopping, or whatever it is that makes them feel happy and relaxed. That thing that they would never give up, then that is the thing that's an idol. And if I sit around longing for romance, instead of longing for God, I put romance ahead of my Lord. Do you see how that makes it an idol?"

"Kinda."

"God said to have no other gods before Him. He wasn't just talking about the gods of the Old Testament, the Amorites and parasites, and all that."

Toni giggled when her mom said parasites. She was pretty sure that wasn't what the people were called in the Bible.

"In today's world, we don't have that so much as we have other things, things that we feel like we can't live without. It could even be politics. We're passionate about politics, or football, scream at the TV set and not miss a game, or cooking, decorating, things that we spend hours searching the Internet for, writing posts about, or taking pictures of. Wanting the perfect thing, we get so passionate about those things, and yet when it comes to God, we're lukewarm. If that. Sometimes we don't even think about Him at all. We definitely have idols in our lives that we need to give up."

"Are you saying that my desire to have a dad is an idol?"

"I can't say that for sure. Only you know your heart. You and God. Do you want a dad more than you want God?"

"I can touch a dad. I don't even know if God is real."

"Some things we just have to take on faith. You have to decide, make a decision as to whether or not you're going to believe He is. As for me, all I have to do is go outside at night and look at the stars, think about how carefully the world is put together, and then you have your science book that tells you it all happened by an explosion. I can't think of the last thing that was carefully put together by an explosion."

Toni smiled. She knew her mom was being sarcastic. Explosions didn't form things that worked in perfect time. Explosions didn't create, they destroyed.

"Are you saying my science textbook is lying to me?"

"You know I am. We've talked about that before."

"Yeah. I know."

"But the biggest reason I know God is real is because He's here with me. I know He is. His spirit bears witness with my spirit. When you're saved, the Spirit of God comes to live inside of you and will help you to live right. It will help me to do the right thing, it will give me the wisdom to make the right decisions, and He will make you feel guilty when you're doing something wrong. In fact, it will be so hard you can barely do it, because God can't stand sin."

"Yeah. Like my conscience."

"Exactly. But your conscience can be seared. The Holy Spirit's voice will get softer and softer if you keep ignoring it. So you ignore Him at your peril. But, like I was saying, that's another reason that I know God is real. He's right here." Her mom patted her chest.

Toni kind of knew what she was talking about. She felt that. Like this afternoon when she was making Marry Me Chicken with her friends, she knew she shouldn't have been doing it without her mom's permission, but she was hoping it would work out anyway. After all, it worked out for Sorrell and Merritt. But after the last debacle, she knew her mom wouldn't want her to do it again.

"So you think I ought to just give up looking for a dad?"

"I think that might be the best idea."

"The old coots were helping me, Mr. Marshall and his friends."

"You think they're going to be disappointed?"

"They might be. We... We were going to talk to them tonight, when you called me home."

"Do you want to go out and let them know that you're not going to be involved in any more schemes like you were this evening?"

"Do you mind?"

"Not at all. Once you go do that, then we can talk some more before we go to bed, okay?"

"I'm sorry, Mom. I didn't mean to make you have a terrible evening."

"It's okay. I... I figured out someone I definitely don't ever want to marry. So you helped me. Technically."

"If you say so." Toni laughed a little, although she was still sad. Sad because her plan hadn't worked out, but also sad because she made her mom miserable for an evening. It wasn't hard to tell with the pinched look around her face and the way her eyes just seemed tired.

She didn't look like she had a fun evening. She looked like she endured, the way she endured her work sometimes.

She claimed to enjoy it, but Toni knew it was hard for her. Her boss was very demanding, and she kind of thought that sometimes her mom wished she could quit.

Probably that was part of being an adult. That's what her mom said anyway. But still, Toni would like to see her not have so much pressure.

Maybe instead of trying to find her mom a husband, she should try to find a job herself, so she could help support her mom, and her mom wouldn't have to work so hard.

"I'll be back before eight o'clock," she promised her mom as she got up off the couch and walked to the door.

They were meeting at the diner after it closed, which Miss Jane had said they could do.

When Toni walked in, Merritt and Sorrell were already sitting with Mr. Marshall, Mr. Blaze, and Mr. Junior.

"Did you get in a lot of trouble?" Sorrell asked, standing up and coming toward her.

"No. Not a lot." She hugged her friend, and then she said, "I hate disappointing Mom. That was the worst part of everything. She was sad and tired."

Mr. Blaze said, "Come on, sit down. We can get some ice cream, Miss Jane said it would be okay as long as we washed our dishes. TikTok isn't exactly helpful helping people to meet up, is it, Mr. Marshall?"

Toni wasn't sure what that was about, but she took it from that comment that they weren't going to be mad at her.

"My mom said that she would prefer if I just stopped altogether. She wants us to allow the Lord to handle everything. She said that me getting a dad has become an idol in my life, and I need to let it go."

"But it's just a goal, a dream."

"Sometimes your goals and dreams become more important to you than doing what God wants you to do. Mom didn't exactly say that, but I know that's what she meant." Toni might not have agreed with her mom completely, but when she had to explain to her friends, it made a lot more sense. If she trusted God, she had to let Him direct her life, and she couldn't let her expectations of what her life should look like cloud her enjoyment of what her life actually was.

# Chapter 15

"You can sit there and talk, I'll grab some ice cream," Marshall said as he got up from the booth where Blaze and Junior sat across from Sorrell, Merritt, and Toni.

He felt terrible for Toni who hadn't had a good evening.

She'd been so excited about finding a single man and about having the Marry Me Chicken. She had hoped it would work on her mom.

Maybe he should suggest she use Billy next time.

But no, she insisted that she just wanted to let the Lord handle everything.

That didn't sit quite right with Mr. Marshall, but what did he know? He met someone online, but she'd ghosted him. Ghosted. That was a new word that the kids used.

Miss Agnes had sounded like a really interesting lady, but when he'd invited her to come visit him, giving her his address, she'd turned him down. And she hadn't been interested in giving out hers.

Glancing out the window as he walked across the floor, he stopped short.

There was an orange car sitting right outside of the diner. Well, orange except for the green fenders.

But the really amazing thing was the hair color of the woman who got out of the car.

It matched the car.

Streaks of orange and green.

He'd never seen hair that color in his life before. And he'd been to New York City.

The woman walked with the gait of a middle-aged woman, but for some reason, he thought she was older.

Maybe it was the frail shoulders.

Interested, he walked to the door. She wouldn't be coming in, since the sign said closed, but if he could help this woman, he was definitely going to.

"Don't forget about our ice cream," Blaze hollered from his seat in the corner booth.

"Get yourself ice cream if you want. I've got a damsel in distress who needs rescuing."

With that, he pushed the door open and walked out to the sidewalk.

He wasn't sure whether she was a damsel in distress or just a damsel. Either way, he was going to help with whatever she needed and make up something if she didn't need it.

"Welcome to Sweet Water. I'm Marshall."

The woman turned, and her brows rose. "You're Marshall. Of TikTok fame."

"That's me." They had a couple of videos go viral on TikTok, and while the excitement had died down, and they hadn't had any luck with any other videos, there still was the occasional person who was behind the eight ball, so to speak, and saw their videos, and came to check them out.

"Then is that the Sweet Water diner?" the woman asked.

"It is. I missed your name."

"You didn't miss it. I didn't give it to you, because I'm not sure I trust you yet." The woman lifted her chin, as though challenging him.

"Why wouldn't you trust me? I live in a small town in North Dakota. We're not exactly crawling with serial killers and other vermin around here."

"I'll be the judge of that. I live in a small town in Idaho, and there are unsavory characters everywhere."

"Idaho?" Marshall's ears perked up more than what they were already. "Are you Miss Agnes?"

"I might be."

"I thought you said if you went somewhere, you wouldn't go by yourself. You'd bring a friend."

"Well, I had to leave one of my friends in Good Grief, because she decided she was tired of being single, kidnapped a potential husband, and got arrested for it. I told her if she was going to tie someone up, she ought to do it to someone other than the police chief's father. But some people just don't pay attention to common sense."

"Yeah. That's common sense."

"And my other friend is still parked out on the lawn of her favorite narrator. Even though he's explained to her several times that she's too old for him, she accuses him of being age biased. I told her that I thought that he looks much younger than what he actually is because he has a makeup artist who does his makeup before he's on camera every day, also a hairdresser and a wardrobe person. At least one of each. Maybe more, I don't know. Anyway, he looks like he's about forty, but I'm pretty sure he's at least fifty-one. If not a year or two older. Anyway, she has her heart set on being a cougar and wants to believe that he's forty. And no matter what anyone says to her, she will not be dissuaded."

"I like a woman who knows her worth," Marshall said, nodding. He wasn't sure who this friend was, but he could admire persistence.

"Well then, you should like me, because I know my heart. I got your message on TikTok, and I decided that I was going to come see you. If I like you, I might marry you." The woman nodded her head decisively. "I do have to warn you that I've been involved in a risqué calendar and nude pictures of me are tacked up all over the walls in rooms of octogenarians everywhere."

"Really?" Far from dissuading him, that perked his interests. He didn't actually believe there were nude pictures of her. But maybe pictures of her feet. That's probably what she meant. He looked down. They were covered in sensible shoes, but he could just see them in high heels, crossed and leaning against a rock on which a wineglass sat at sunset.

Yeah. That would be a good picture.

"All right. I'll marry you."

"I haven't decided whether I want to get married or not."

"This is going to come as a shock to you, but you're not getting any younger, neither am I. We don't have time to sit around and think about things anymore. If we're going to get married, we'd better get it done."

"First of all, I'm new in town, and I haven't even made it to the home where I'm staying for the night."

"Where is that? I'll take you to it."

"I have a friend who helped to write a story about Good Grief. She put us on the map. She was originally from Texas but moved up here chasing a story, I believe, but rumor has it in Good Grief that she found someone from her past and is slowly romancing him. I've discussed things with her, not her romance, but accommodations. She said her aunt has a room I can stay in. Perhaps you know Eliza Walton?"

"I sure do. And she lives with her Aunt April. Just up the street here a couple blocks. Good thing you're not wearing those high heels you got all those pictures taken in, because you probably wouldn't want to walk up the street in those."

"High heels?"

"You know, for the risqué calendar."

"Oh, I wasn't wearing anything," Miss Agnes said, and this time, Marshall wasn't sure whether he believed her or not. Unfortunately, he'd already told her he would marry her, and he could hardly go back on his word. But if there were nude pictures, actual nude pictures of her floating around, they were going to have to have a long discussion about whether or not she was going to be able to continue her outlandish activities after their nuptials.

"Do you have a suitcase?"

"I have six suitcases. However, I only need three of them for this evening. I'll wait while you get them out."

Marshall grinned. "How about you hand me the keys, and I'll take this beauty for a spin around town before I park in front of Miss April's house. After that, if you promise that you'll kiss me good night, I might take your suitcases out."

"I don't kiss men I don't know, so you'd better do a lot of talking on our trip around town." She tilted her head, as though thinking about something. "Maybe I should put kissing a man I don't know on my bucket list."

She narrowed her eyes, looking at him, before she stepped forward, grabbed his head, and pressed her lips against his.

He was too shocked to respond for the first couple of seconds, then he didn't hesitate, grabbing her around the waist, putting another arm around her shoulders, and pressing his lips into hers.

If he was only going to have one opportunity to kiss a woman with hair that was both orange and green, he certainly wasn't going to turn it down.

From somewhere far away, he thought he heard a moo, probably from Billy. He wasn't sure.

Regardless, he could almost hear wedding bells.

Who needed TikTok?

# Chapter 16

"**J**une, honey, if he cheated, you can leave."

June sat across from Rebecca Bailey, the counselor that she had made an appointment with in Rockerton.

Her eyes pricked with tears. She didn't want to leave her husband. She didn't want to be divorced. She didn't want to not be married anymore.

When she'd said vows thirty years ago, she had every intention of keeping them. For better or for worse. Wasn't this worse?

"You don't want to stay with someone you can't trust."

No. Of course not.

June nodded, but her mind was reeling. She already knew that. She didn't come here to be told what she already knew. She wanted to find out something different. Something that would unlock the key in her mind to make it so that it felt right to divorce her husband or that she knew what steps to take if she wasn't going to.

"What if I decide to stay?" she asked.

"You might as well be prepared for him to continue to lie to you and to cheat on you as well. I would get tested for STDs regularly."

The counselor didn't pull any punches.

June swallowed hard. STDs. She shouldn't even be thinking about something like that. She'd been faithful to the same man for thirty years. STDs shouldn't even be in her vocabulary.

"I'll pray for you. You can pray for yourself. You could have people praying for you. But a man who is a narcissist is not going to change without major intervention from Jesus. Narcissists don't change."

Rebecca emphasized those last three words. June had figured out as much from reading on the Internet, but she wanted to believe that there was something she could do that would make it so that her marriage was salvageable.

She didn't want to have to depend on someone else. Wayne wasn't the same person that she'd married thirty years ago. He was worse. He'd spent thirty years bossing her around, expecting her to bow to his every wish, and she had. She'd been obedient and submissive, just like the Bible commanded, and this was what she got.

"Do you have any advice for me?" she asked Rebecca, who was looking at her with compassion, but there was also determination in the woman's eyes. She had seen this type of thing before, and she knew that there was no hope for June's marriage. At least no earthly hope.

"That's my advice. Leave him. He's never going to change, he's always going to cheat, he's never going to be a truthful, honest, trustworthy person who cares about you. June, if you ever get sick, he's not going to take care of you."

June already knew that. She hadn't told her counselor that she had cancer last year. And that her husband had barely come for her surgery, and that was pretty much all he'd shown up for.

"But if we don't make this about you," Rebecca said gently, "let's make this about Jesus. The Bible says that you are to serve other people like they're Jesus. Right?"

"Exactly. That's exactly what it says." And that's what had gotten her through her marriage. She had had to think to herself, sometimes on a daily basis, that she was serving Wayne like he was Jesus. That she would be rewarded for her service. That it wasn't in vain and maybe, just maybe, someday Wayne would come to Christ.

And all her service would be worthwhile. It would be if it kept even one person out of hell.

"So serving, obeying, submitting. That's all part of your marriage and part of something that's biblical. But it's never going to make a marriage that is a picture of Christ and the church, because it's only a one-way street. It's all you serving and loving and giving, and you never get anything in return."

Rebecca steepled her hands on her desk and leaned forward.

"I admire you. I admire you for being able to do that for thirty years. To love that man with your actions and get nothing in return for it. There aren't a lot of people who would be able to do that."

Rebecca's words were sincere, and they made June feel a little bit validated.

"But he cheated. That changes things."

She emphasized the last three words. Then she sat in silence for a little bit.

"You made a covenant on the day that you got married. To be true to each other. To be faithful to each other. You pledged your lives to each other, to have no one else. That was a covenant between the two of you and God. When he cheated, he brought someone else into the covenant, and he broke it. He broke the covenant with you. You are not bound by that any longer because it is no longer in force. That leaves you free to go." She blew out a breath and shook her head a little. "Even Jesus said except for fornication. That is the only biblical reason that Jesus gives for divorce. Now he said Moses said because of the hardness of your hearts, but Jesus didn't agree with him. That's not a good reason. But in the case of fornication, it is okay to get divorced."

June sat listening, her heart crying in her chest. She didn't want her marriage vows to be broken. She didn't want to have an excuse to get out of her marriage. Yeah, it would have been nice if Wayne could have been kind to her over the years. Loving, encouraging, supportive. But she learned to live with it anyway. Just because she said she would.

She didn't exactly dream of celebrating her fiftieth wedding anniversary, but she had wanted to make it to that point. She wanted to be married for fifty years. For a lifetime. That was what she meant when she had made vows to her husband as a young bride.

She and Rebecca talked a little more, then she got up and left, paying at the front desk before she went out.

She hadn't made up her mind as to what she needed to do, but she knew one thing for sure. She needed to talk to her children.

She called them on the way home. Veronica was in college, the other two had graduated. They all agreed to meet at the old white church in Sweet Water.

Her two boys would have to take off work, but while she wouldn't normally ask for her children to do that, they understood that it was something very serious when she did.

The church was never locked, and she made it there first. She walked in and sat in the back pew.

Pews weren't exactly designed for a four-way conversation, but they'd make it work. There wasn't really any place else in the world where she felt as comfortable as she did in the church. Walking into it soothed her heart in some way she couldn't explain.

Veronica arrived first, her brows knitted, her expression concerned. "Mom? Is the cancer back?"

June smiled as reassuringly as she could. "No. No one's life is in danger. I just have a major decision to make, and I wanted to discuss it with you and your brothers before I did."

"It's about Dad, isn't it?"

"Can we talk about something else until your brothers get here?" June asked as her daughter settled down in the pew beside her, putting her arm around her and pulling her close. The roles reversed.

It felt good to have someone's care and concern. It wasn't something she was used to, though.

The boys arrived together. Not boys anymore. Men. They'd grown and had their own families, and June was excited that she would be getting a grandchild in the spring.

"Mom? Are you okay?" Wayne, Jr., nicknamed Chuck by everyone, came in with the same concern on his face that Veronica had had on hers.

"I'm fine. No cancer." She answered the cancer question before it was even asked.

Their faces visibly relaxed.

Chris was less vocal than her other two children but every bit as concerned. He almost smiled as he realized that they weren't talking about another health scare.

"It's about Dad," Chuck said easily as he settled. He didn't seem worried or concerned that there might be something happening with his father.

They didn't have a great relationship, because Chuck had idolized his dad clear up into his teens, when he finally realized that his dad was never going to want to have anything to do with him.

Their relationship had been rocky after that, with Wayne so many times not even acting like a father. June didn't understand how a man could have kids and act like they were almost strangers. The way he treated his boys over the years had been a major source of contention between the two of them, with June trying not to take sides but trying to gently suggest that maybe Wayne could take time away from some of his hobbies to spend time with his boys or take his boys with him, if it had to be that way.

Wayne hadn't been interested until the boys were old enough to do what he did, and by then, they weren't interested.

"Yes. It's about your dad."

She had debated over and over again how much to tell her children. How much to hide. How much she should try to keep to herself to protect Wayne and any possibility that he might have a relationship with his children in the future.

"Dad cheated on you." Chris's words were spoken flatly. Not even like he was guessing, but like he knew and figured she had just found out.

"Do you know that for sure?"

"One of the guys I worked with said that his dad was out with his mom for their weekly date night."

June tried not to flinch. She didn't have a weekly date night with her husband. She wasn't even sure her husband wanted to date her. He certainly didn't act like he wanted to spend time with her.

"They saw Dad with another woman. I questioned him, whether or not he was sure, but they used to work together, and my buddy's dad knew Dad and didn't have any doubt. The woman he was with wasn't you."

"All right. Yeah, that isn't the one I heard, but that's what I wanted to talk to you guys about. He cheated, and I'm thinking about divorce."

"I don't think any of us will blame you if you get divorced, Mom. You put up with more than any woman should have to put up with from Dad. He's been a jerk the whole time I've known him. He hasn't changed or gotten better, and you've taken the brunt of it over the years. You deserve a shot at happiness." Chuck's words were not sad or aghast. He didn't seem the slightest bit upset that his parents may not stay together.

"I appreciate that, Chuck. Chris?"

"I'm with Chuck. Dad's a jerk. I don't know how you stayed with him so long. I couldn't wait to get out of the house. And it wasn't because of you. I'd have lived there until I was married with you. Not that we agree on everything, you're just...nice."

"Veronica?" June asked, looking at her daughter who did not seem as sure as the boys. She was younger, first of all, and it seemed like the cheating idea had shaken her a little bit more.

"Dad cheated?" she asked, looking at June, then glancing at her brothers who both nodded. "Why didn't you guys tell me?" she asked, a little bit of anger seeping into her tone as she eyed the men sitting in the pew ahead of them.

"I wanted to tell Mom. But I didn't have pictures, I didn't have proof, I didn't even know for sure whether he was cheating or just, I don't know, taking some other woman out to eat. I suppose it's kind of wishful thinking to think that nothing happened afterward, or before, whatever. But until I had actual proof in hand, I couldn't go to Mom and tear her world down."

Veronica nodded, agreeing with that. "You know for sure?"

June took a breath. She didn't want to go into details. But she also needed details in order to believe. "I visited the wife of someone who used to work with your dad. We were actually quite close. They knew that he cheated years ago, and they thought I knew too. When I spoke with her not long ago, she was shocked that I didn't know, and very apologetic for letting the cat out of the bag, so to speak. She didn't tell me out of spite or vindictiveness and actually didn't tell me on purpose at all. That makes it very believable, even if the story hadn't been believable, which it had."

June hated that she was talking about her husband to her kids and dragging him down. But at the same time, they were his actions that they were discussing. She wasn't making anything up to make him look bad. They were just telling each other what they'd seen him do. If he hadn't done it, he wouldn't look bad.

"If Dad cheated on you, Mom, you definitely need to leave him. There's no way you should stay with someone like that." She closed her mouth, looked away for a moment, and pressed her lips together before she looked back at her mom. "Mom, if there was a relationship worth salvaging, if Dad were a nice guy who just made a mistake, if this was something that Dad did a long time ago and was apologetic for, but... He's not exactly someone worth fighting for."

"He's someone God loves," June said softly.

"I know. I know God loves him, but he's made you miserable for years."

"I'm a better person because I had to learn to love him and get along with him. I wouldn't be the Christian I am today if I hadn't stayed with your dad and tried to make our marriage work."

"That's a good point. Maybe this is God saying enough is enough, because all of these things are coming out."

June had thought of that. That maybe God had given her a trial, and now she was released from it. The thing was, she wasn't sure she wanted out of her marriage.

"You guys realize you will no longer have a mom and a dad who are together. My grandkids, your children," she looked at Chuck whose wife was expecting in the spring, "won't go visit their grandparents. They'll just go visit their grandmother and then go visit their grandfather."

"That's wishful thinking, Mom. Dad isn't going to be the slightest bit interested in seeing my kid. He wasn't interested in seeing me. I can't imagine that he'd be chomping at the bit to see my child."

"Mom, the last time I called Dad, I wanted to ask him what kind of tires he thought I should get for my car. I hadn't talked to him in a couple of months. But instead of him sounding like he was happy to hear from me, he said he was too busy to talk and that he'd call me back later. That was about six weeks ago. And he still hasn't called me back," Chris said casually, his tone informational, but it made June's heart bleed.

She loved her children, and she wanted them to have a dad who loved them. Not a dad who didn't seem like he cared about them at all. He treated strangers better than he treated his family. And her.

Divorce wasn't going to change that or make it any better. It wasn't going to help. Wasn't going to fix anything.

"I'm sorry, Chris. I wish... I wish things were different." What she really wished was that she would have made a smarter decision when she was younger, but she couldn't go back and change it.

"I'd say, Veronica, that you don't want Mom's advice on your future husband, because she is terrible at picking a good man, but I think that maybe her experience has given her wisdom, and she'd be the perfect person to ask." Chuck patted her forearm, and his hand slipped down and wrapped around hers and squeezed.

She smiled at him, a sad smile but also one of relief. He wasn't blaming her. He wasn't looking at her and thinking that there was a problem with her or that she had done something wrong to cause all of this.

The kids knew how hard she had worked to make a home for them, to do her very best for them, and yes, that even included disciplining them the times they needed it.

As they got older, they had laughed at some of the things they had done wrong and thanked June for not letting them get away with anything.

But there had never been happy family times with Wayne. He couldn't be bothered to sit around with the family and talk. He had better things to do.

"Why did you stay with him so long?" Veronica asked.

"The Bible says the only reason for divorce is fornication. I guess... If he had abused us in any way, I suppose I would have left, but I probably wouldn't have divorced him."

Veronica nodded, looking away. Maybe she wished her childhood had been different.

June wanted to stop that thinking.

"I've been thinking for a while that I made a mistake. That I chose poorly when I was younger, but I know that God knows and allowed it. That our experiences shape us. They help us to create a better life for our children, if we put the things that we learned to use. You two will be better husbands and fathers because you saw what your dad did, and you know that you want to do things differently. Veronica, you'll be smarter in your choice for a husband, because I can tell you all the lies I heard before I got married and the things I believed, and how I should have lined up what he said with what he did, and saw that it didn't fit. But I wasn't old enough or wise enough to do that, and I was fooled. So not to talk badly about him specifically, but in general, we can take what we have with our lives right now and make it turn out for the best. That's our choice."

She looked at each of her three children. She had so much fun with them growing up. She enjoyed every second with them, well, except when they were fighting. It had been hard. Of course it had been hard, since she had been like a single mom with three kids. But they survived, and she was pleased with the way her children had turned out. They weren't perfect, of course, neither was she, but they were people who knew that they could learn and grow and become better.

"Did you confront Dad about him cheating?" Chris asked almost as though he had just thought of it.

"I did. He told me I was stupid, you know the drill." June didn't want to dwell on the negative. "I wouldn't have moved forward without saying something to him. It's not fair he doesn't know that I know."

"It's not fair that he cheated in the first place," Chuck said, and there was a lot of anger in his tone.

"If he would have apologized. If he could have said I'm sorry, I was wrong, let's work on this, but...of course he didn't." She closed her eyes and shook her head. "I was kind of hoping that would happen. But no. He denied it, called me a liar, called them a liar, etc."

She didn't need to get into all the details, but the kids already knew what their dad was like. They'd experienced him growing up.

They'd been called liars when they had been telling the truth, and he had been lying.

"What are you going to do, Mom?" Veronica asked, squeezing her shoulders.

"I guess I'm going to keep praying about it. I really don't know."

"If you need to get divorced, I don't blame you at all. I don't think any of the three of us do." Chuck looked over at his two siblings, then nodded back at his mom as they shook their heads.

"Thanks. I guess that's good to know. I... I don't know what to do. But I guess I'll just keep praying and asking God to show me. Because the one thing that I don't want to do is step out of what God wants me to do. I want to do whatever He has for me. Whether that is staying with someone, and just praying for them, treating them like they're Jesus...or something else."

June sighed, because the idea of spending the next thirty years of her life the way she had spent the last thirty years was a little depressing. She wanted to be loved and cherished and romanced. Not necessarily like a little girl dreams of being romanced and swept off her feet by a handsome prince, but just... Just to be with someone who enjoyed her company and wanted to spend time with her. Who cared about her and hoped that everything was okay with her.

Who held her hand when she was sick, and who didn't have a problem making it to the hospital to be her ride home. Who didn't want her to go to rehab but wanted her to be with him so he could take care of her.

That was never going to happen in her relationship, not without a miracle.

"I think it's a good idea for us all to pray about this," Chuck said as he looked around his siblings. "I don't think it would hurt to start right now."

They all bowed their heads, and Chuck prayed over them. It warmed June's heart to hear her child praying. Praying for all of them. Praying for God's will, and letting his love for Jesus show.

She supposed that's what she got out of her marriage, three children who loved the Lord and wanted to serve Him. And that was worth it. That wouldn't have happened if they hadn't seen her do her best to put what she read in the Bible into practice in her life, even though it had never been easy.

They chatted for a while, and then they left the church together, Chuck wrapping his arm around June as they descended the stairs of the church.

"I didn't want to say this in front of the other two," he said low into her ear, "but Candy," that was his wife, "and I talked about when the baby comes. She expressed doubts already about allowing our child to be around Dad. She's seen the way he treats us and you, and she's afraid that he's going to do the same thing to her child. She asked me if it would be okay if we said that he's not allowed to see our baby. I... I didn't want to go that far, but I respect what she said. And I figured you'd understand too."

That made June's heart sink. But she couldn't argue with Chuck. Or with Candy. They wanted to do the best for their child, and hadn't she just been thinking that she wished she would have chosen someone else? That she wished her children had a better childhood, even though she'd done the very best she could for them.

"I understand. I can't fight about it. You need to make the best decision for your baby."

"I didn't want to hurt you, Mom. I guess, when you said you were thinking about getting divorced, I thought in my heart that it would make things a lot easier for me and for our children, if I didn't have to wonder whether Dad was going to be around before I came to visit. There's just a lot of problems that that would solve. Not that I'm trying to talk you into getting divorced."

"No. I understand. I can't say that I blame you. I will definitely take that into consideration, but I don't feel like you're trying to talk me into anything."

"I'm not. I truly do want you just to do what God wants you to do. Nothing more, nothing less."

June looked up at him and smiled, and they finished walking down the stairs together.

She didn't know what she was going to do, but she knew one thing, God would never fail her or forsake her, and she could depend on Him, even if she couldn't depend on her husband.

# Chapter 17

"The x-rays have shown that your leg has healed better than we expected. I would say another two weeks off your leg, and you will gradually be able to start putting weight on it again."

The doctor looked once more at the x-rays, nodding his head as though confirming his diagnosis, and then turned back to look at Hines and then at Eliza who was sitting in the chair beside the examining table.

"Do either of you have any questions?"

Eliza shook her head, and Hines shrugged.

"Unless there's any way we can get it to go faster?" He couldn't help it. He had been off his feet for four weeks and couldn't wait to be able to start walking again. His arm he wasn't as concerned about, but the doctors already told him that it was healing as well.

"You're already going faster than most people. I think you want to be grateful, and don't push it. Because you can set yourself back pretty easily." The doctor raised his brows. "Anything else?"

They shook their heads.

They chatted a bit more with the doctor, then shook hands, and he left, closing the door behind him, leaving Hines and Eliza alone.

"That's great news!" Eliza said, grinning with excitement. There was no doubt that she was rooting for him to get better.

There was a part of him that wondered if it was because she was eager to get back to her life. After all, the sooner he was able to get around, the sooner she wouldn't need to be around him anymore.

Every once in a while, he acted like he couldn't do something he knew he could, just so she'd do it for him and not think that he was getting too independent.

There was a part of him that had gotten used to having her hanging around and didn't want her to go.

"I can't wait to be able to walk. It's nice that you and I can go out and feed now, and Miller doesn't have to come anymore, but it's always difficult for me that I'm not able to do everything I want to do."

"It was a happy day when Miller didn't have to come anymore, that's for sure." She smiled, getting her purse and putting the strap over her shoulder.

"Are you sure you don't mind? Sometimes I wonder if I'm not asking too much out of you?"

"I've really been enjoying it. It is cold, and I can't say that I enjoy that, but I love being outside, I love being with the animals, and..." She tilted her head. "I love watching you with the horses. There is just a beauty as you work that is amazing to watch."

Her words made him want to smile like a kindergartner praised for their handwriting. He supposed his chest probably did pop out a little bit, and he said, maybe a little more grumbly than necessary, "Let's go."

He opened the door for her, and she stepped out.

This was the part he hated the most. Once they got back to the exam room, he felt like he was fine, but walking through the hall to and from the waiting room, and the time in the waiting room, were the worst parts of the doctor's visits.

He appreciated the fact that this doctor had allowed him up until this point to have video chat visits.

But they wanted x-rays, and of course they couldn't do that over the computer.

He waited for Eliza to pass through, then hopped out using his crutches, closing the door behind him.

Eliza didn't try to help him, which he was grateful for. He already felt conspicuous and like an object of pity. He didn't need Eliza fussing over him right now.

As much as he enjoyed it at home, he didn't want to appear weak in public.

But he'd barely turned and took a hop, falling in beside Eliza who was waiting for him, when a little boy and his mom came around the corner.

"What's wrong with him?" the boy asked in what seemed like an extremely loud voice, pointing at Hines's face.

"Hush, Tyler. That's not nice."

"What's not nice? He's ugly."

Eliza had stepped aside so the mother and son could pass them in the narrow hall, then she fell into step beside him as his crutches hit the floor rhythmically.

He couldn't wait to get out of there.

He still had to stop at the front desk, and it felt like it took forever for the receptionist to make an appointment for him in another two weeks.

They couldn't get out to the car fast enough, and he barely looked at Eliza as he settled himself in the passenger seat.

Eliza got in the driver's side but sat there for a moment before she turned the key.

"Are you okay?" she asked softly.

"I'm fine."

"It's pretty cold out, but I could have worn a skirt."

"I don't need you to garner just as much negative attention as I do." He tried not to let his words sound bitter, but they were.

"I just thought it might take some of the attention off you."

"What? It's noble for you to sacrifice yourself so that you can keep my delicate, tender feelings from being hurt?"

That's exactly what she was saying, but it sounded stupid when he said it. Why were his feeling so delicate and tender?

"No. Just to have someone beside you experiencing the same thing. Sometimes it's easier when we have someone on our team."

"We're not a team."

Actually he wouldn't mind having Eliza on his team. She'd been faithful, coming every day earlier than he expected and staying until he was ready for bed.

She'd never asked for anything and had done whatever he wanted her to do.

Of course, he wasn't exactly a demanding patient, really only needing help to get in and out of his chair, and honestly, he didn't even need that now.

Still she came. And he appreciated it.

"I'm sorry I made that assumption," she said, starting the car.

"I'm sorry."

His words didn't sound sorry. He sounded belligerent.

He tried again, infusing actual contrition into his words. "Sorry."

"I understand. Mostly."

"No, you don't. Your face still looks normal. As long as you have long pants on, you can pass for a normal person."

"What's so great about being normal?" She narrowed her eyes and looked at him. "Is that really the goal in life? To be normal?"

Her question took him back. Of course he wanted to be normal. He wanted to fit in. He didn't want to stand out like some monster at a petting zoo.

"I mean, normal is average. Right? We don't need to be average. Are we trying to be different? Don't we all want to be different?"

"Not different like this. This is different in a bad way. Different in good ways."

"Who defines that?"

Another good question. What was he doing, depending on the world to make the definitions of what normal was or what beautiful was?

"That's your face. There's nothing you can do about it. Just move forward. Taking what you have, making the best of it. You know, somewhere in the world, there's someone who wishes they had everything that you do."

"So there's one person who has it worse than I do, and I'm supposed to be grateful for that?"

He couldn't help spitting the words out. After all, he didn't need her telling him that he needed to be grateful.

"I'm sure there are a lot of people who would take what you have, everything, and appreciate it. Regardless, you're right. It's not my job to lecture you. And I'm sorry."

"No," he said after a moment. "You're right. I... I reacted badly. I usually react badly. That's why I avoid going out in public. I...don't know what to do, don't know what to say when people are pointing at me and calling me ugly and telling me what an atrocity I am."

"Same thing you do whenever you look normal and people insult you. Our default setting is to get upset. Is to get annoyed, to lash back out." She huffed out a breath. "I don't have so much trouble doing that with people who do that to me anymore. I learned to smile. Be kind. People don't really mean to be mean. And the people who do mean to be mean just need pity, not anger. After all, if they've got that kind of vitriol inside of them that they need to spew it at someone who has obviously been through a traumatic event, then they deserve pity, not anger. But I found myself wanting to grab a hold of that little boy, even though he's just a child and really didn't mean to be nasty, but I wanted to hurt him, because he had hurt you."

Hines froze. He had just been really unkind to her. He told her he didn't want to be on a team with her. Whatever that was. Just to throw words back in her face. And she had responded to his unkindness with kindness, not just telling him how he needed to be but showing him.

He hung his head, his eyes focused on his knees, his heart beating slow as his whole body felt heavy and guilty.

She pulled out of the parking lot and was on the road pointed toward home when he said, "I'm sorry. I owe you another apology. Because you didn't just tell me that I need to be kind to people who are unkind to me, you turned around and were actually kind to me when I was unkind to you. You showed me and lived what you said."

She smiled a little and angled her eyes over to him, tilting her head, then looking back at the road. "I'm sorry. I didn't quite hear that. You mind repeating it?"

"Stop it. That's rude. It was hard enough to apologize the first time."

"I know. I thought maybe you need to practice, so you can do it twice."

"I'm sorry. I was wrong. I react badly, both to that little boy and to you. You were kind to me. And I didn't deserve it. Thank you." He jerked his head. "There. How's that? Twice."

"I'm impressed. I didn't think I was going to get two."

"If you want a third one, just say so. You deserve it."

"No. I really don't. I've had more practice than you have, I'm sure. Although, you're probably right, having the scars on your face makes it much more difficult and obvious, but I do know I didn't use to react well to people when they said things about my legs. Especially when the people who said things were supposed to be my friends. So, maybe when you've had as much practice as I have, you'll react the same way too."

"I don't know. I've been trying to temper my reactions. And it's pretty obvious to me that you spent a lot of time thinking about and working toward being better. I have a lot of ground to catch up on."

They traveled in silence for a bit, and then he said, "You know, it's been a week since you took time off. Why don't you take tomorrow off? You deserve it. For putting up with me."

"I really don't deserve anything, I promise you. But maybe I'll take you up on that offer. My aunt has been after me because she wants to come out to see you again. She's curious about you, and I think she likes you, too. I'm pretty sure she's not going to insult you to your face." She looked over at him with her brows raised, and he took that look to mean that her aunt was the kind of woman who might end up saying things that made him uncomfortable.

It would be good practice for him. So as much as he wanted to take the invitation back, he clamped his lips down around the words and refused to allow himself to back out.

Whether her aunt was an old battle-ax or not, he would face her and do his best to be kind.

What Eliza had said earlier about taking what he had been given and making the most of it came back to him. He wasn't going to be angry at God anymore for his face. He was going to be thankful for his ranch. Thankful for the people in his life who weren't afraid to tell him when he was messing up. People like Eliza.

# Chapter 18

"Oh my goodness! No one can believe that you're actually out at his house every day. You would not believe the people in Sweet Water that didn't even know that Hines Cannon lived here, let alone that he had burned his face saving someone, and that someone is you! You have been the talk of the town recently, girl."

Eliza sat at a table in the Sweet Water diner across from her friend Kenni.

Kenni's gushing made Eliza a little nervous, because she knew that Hines would not laugh. He didn't want people to know that he was a hero who had saved a life. He didn't want the notoriety. And the reason that he lived as a recluse near Sweet Water was because he wanted the privacy.

"I don't think he's going to be happy if he hears that's getting out around town. In fact, I know he's not going to be happy."

"You can't control gossip. And this isn't really gossip. Honestly, the town really cares about him, and you wouldn't believe the people who want to help out now that they know. I mean I'm getting questions every day about whether or not you guys need food or whether they can take anything out or help feed his animals or just people asking what they can do. It's unbelievable."

"Small towns look after each other. And that's a nice thing. But if you want privacy, sometimes it can be grating. And I know that's what Hines wants."

"He knows that's not healthy, right?" Kenni said, and her words didn't sound snobby, they sounded concerned.

"Yeah, but I think when you've been through what he's been through, sometimes it just feels safe. You know?"

"Are you making excuses for him?"

"I am a little bit, aren't I?"

"I think you like him," Kenni said, like she was discovering an ancient secret.

Eliza looked around at the empty diner. Two o'clock in the afternoon wasn't exactly a busy time. "I do. I like him a lot."

"You guys do spend a lot of time together. And you've seen him at his worst."

"I don't know if it's been at his worst, but I've definitely seen him in pain. Frustrated. Angry even."

"You like him anyway?"

"Well, I know that there's such a thing as rescue devotion or whatever it's called where you fall in love with the person who rescues you? Or doctor devotion where you fall in love with the doctor who took care of you or whatever, but I admit I've always had a little bit of a crush on him. Even though I didn't know him at all. Just the idea of someone coming in and moving a burning beam from off of you so that you can get out from underneath it and saving your life, how can that not be..."

"Romantic!" Kenni said, laughing.

"I know. But when I first met him, seeing what he was like, it wasn't love at first sight or anything like that. I was actually a little disappointed."

"Because he was so angry and mean?"

"I hate to call him angry or mean but...yeah. He wasn't nice. A little rude. Just not the man of character that I'd always envisioned, you know?"

"Yeah, I know. We all want that." Kenni moved her napkin around the table. "We want people to be what we envision in our mind and not what they actually are in reality. Sometimes the two are so far apart that it's laughable."

Eliza figured Kenni probably knew what she was talking about since she had been married to a prince and had been a princess for a while. She probably was used to people thinking that she was something that she was not, glamorous and perfect.

"But I've been there every day for a few weeks, and he's funny. And kind. He's so good with the horses that he rescues. Patient and affectionate. Watching him work with the horses makes me feel like the man that he is isn't the same as the one he shows the world. That there is someone amazing in there, and that's the man I'm falling for."

"You won't know if you never see that man."

"Exactly. He only has two more weeks until he can start putting weight on his foot. We were just at the doctor's yesterday. And in one way, I'm dreading for the two weeks to be over, because I love going out to see him every day. Then on the other hand, I'm looking forward to it. Because I know if I don't soon get out of there, I'm going to have myself totally in love with a man that might not even exist."

"But he might. Why don't you see if you can find out?"

"How do I do that?"

"I don't know. Talk to him? Do something with him? Or maybe...work with his horses with him?"

Eliza nodded. Those were all good ideas. Maybe she could figure something out. "But it's not going to do me any good if he doesn't feel the same way about me."

"Eliza, how could anyone know you and not love you?"

Lots of people had no problem doing that, but Eliza didn't correct her friend. She just laughed, and they started talking about something else.

# Chapter 19

Hines stood at the sink washing dishes.

Eliza was cleaning up the meal they had and putting the food away.

Soon she'd come over, grab a tea towel, and start drying.

How could he get her to stay?

That had been the question that had been going over and over in his mind for the last week. Ever since the doctor's appointment. When he realized that her excitement that he would be walking again soon could possibly be because she would no longer have to come to his house.

He hadn't come up with any plan. Other than break the other leg, which he really didn't want to have to do. He wanted her to stay, but he wanted her to stay and him be whole. At least as whole as he could be.

She insisted that his face didn't matter to her, and she had acted like it hadn't. Kind of unbelievably.

"So you said you weren't married?" As soon as the words left his lips, he realized how strange they sounded, landing in the silence of the kitchen.

They'd been joking about telling Alice not to include Brussels sprouts in any of the food that she cooked ever again, since neither one of them liked them. But then they'd ended up having a competition over who could eat the most Brussels sprouts, even though they both hated them. Which was crazy, but they'd both been laughing so hard by the time they were done eating that they could barely stand up.

He couldn't remember ever having a more fun meal with anyone. Which was completely shocking, considering the meal consisted of him eating more Brussels sprouts than he had ever eaten in his life before.

By the time he'd eaten the twelfth one, he'd almost gotten to the point where he was beginning to think he might be able to actually start to like them.

Crazy.

That's what Eliza did to him.

Now, with him asking that question, the camaraderie in the room disappeared, and confusion or maybe suspicion took its place.

"I was married once. It...was a mistake. He left me, and I decided that wasn't a mistake I was going to repeat. So I didn't." She lifted her shoulders, shrugging like it didn't matter, as she grabbed a tea towel and took the plate from his hand. "You know, you could be married."

He barked out a laugh, short and sarcastic.

"I'm serious. The person you fall in love with, you're going to fall in love with her because she will love you the way you are."

"I think that's a fairy tale," he finally said, chagrined that he had laughed at her but knowing his humor was justified. No one was going to fall in love with him. He had to break a leg just to get someone to stay.

"I think it's not," she said easily, not afraid to disagree with him. He liked that. He could be a little scary at times, not just because he looked scary, but because his personality had become that sarcastic, almost rude in self-defense.

"I guess you have to explain that for me."

"Well, even someone with a normal-looking face, and you know how I feel about normal, isn't going to find someone to fall in love with them if they don't put themselves out there and take a few risks now and then. Everyone has to take risks."

"I don't disagree with that. I took a risk when I went into that burning school and moved the beam off of your burning body."

"And then you never took a risk again?"

"I never felt it was worth it."

That was true. But maybe, maybe he found someone for whom the risk was worth it.

"Would you like to go see the horses after we're done with the dishes?" Normally after supper, they settled down into chairs and chatted back and forth, sometimes playing a game, sometimes just talking, a couple of times they'd watched a movie together. But usually their evenings were quiet.

"I'd love to. I'd love to see Sassy. It's always fun to see them at a time when they're not expecting to."

Since she'd been helping him feed, she'd been seeing Sassy morning and evening.

"I know what you're saying. See what she looks like when she's all bedded down for the night."

"Yeah. Surprise her a little. I wish there was a treat or something we could get her to take."

"When I'm able to walk again, that's what I'll start doing first. To get her to come to me, if not let me touch her, just let me feed her out of my hand."

"Can we try that tonight?"

He almost said no. It was on the tip of his tongue. But a voice stopped him, saying that if he was able to get Eliza to fall in love with the horses, maybe she would come out so she could continue seeing them. He was desperate to get her to want to spend time with him or to get to be able to see her after he was able to walk. Maybe this was the key.

"I think it's a good idea. Most horses will take treats, but some never learned to. So I think we're best going out with a couple handfuls of feed. She's probably not going to let us pet her tonight." So much of being patient was realizing that things might not happen at the speed which they wanted them to and to be okay with that. "She might not even come over to us tonight, although she is used to us feeding her."

"I've noticed that she's been putting on weight," Eliza said as she set a second plate on top of the first one and then grabbed some silverware to dry off.

"She has. She is looking a lot better than she was. Believe it or not, she's not the skinniest horse I've ever had."

Eliza shivered. "I don't even want to know about that. That just...turns my stomach that a horse could suffer so much."

"Any animal. Dogs, cats... There's a lot of suffering in the world."

He didn't even go into the wild animals that he'd seen. Of course there wasn't much he could do to help, and sometimes he didn't want to. Possums, for example, carried a disease that could devastate a horse. He didn't really want them around anyway.

"I don't think it's ever fun to see anything suffer. But I do think that there is a strength to be found as you go through suffering. But it's our choice to find it."

"Sometimes we learn things without our consent." He smiled a little at that.

"I think some people go through school like that."

"I admit, there were a few classes where I learned things despite myself." They laughed together.

He let the water out of the sink, and she folded her towel up and put it over the handle of the oven.

"It's going to be colder with the sun down, so be sure you dress warm." He knew she didn't need the warning, but he felt like he needed to give it to her anyway. After all, they were both from Texas and not used to the kind of cold that North Dakota could deliver.

"I appreciate the reminder. Every time I go out, it seems to surprise me. Even though I bundle up tight, I get cold. You wouldn't have that kind of thing in Texas."

"Only a couple of days of the year, and that was, you know, thirty degrees feels cold."

"Exactly."

She didn't try to help him, although he knew she kept her eye on him watching to see if she could. He appreciated that. She seemed to give him the perfect amount of space. Not that she never irritated him, and not that he had never needed something when she had been around, but he wasn't constantly tripping over her or wishing she would be more attentive.

They seemed to go together well.

"You know, what you said about us being a team?" he said as he used his crutches to hop to the door where she waited for him.

"Yeah?"

"I kind of feel like we do work well together. I've... Since I said what I did to you, saying that we weren't a team, I regretted it. I just wanted to say that."

He stopped beside her, but she made no move to open the door.

"Now I wonder what made you change your mind about that?"

"Are you trying to make me admit that I was wrong again?"

"I think you just did."

"True."

"And I was wondering why?"

"I guess I don't know. I guess... I guess I really enjoyed our time working together. I don't think I've ever worked with anyone that I have more fun with. And it's not just working, supper tonight was probably the best time I've ever had, and that is pretty surprising considering it included Brussels sprouts."

She stuck her tongue out, and he laughed.

But once her laughter faded, she grew serious again.

"I could say the same thing about you. I really did have a good time at supper. The laughter and the fun. I... I knew that was a part of you, but it's fun to see it. And it's really great to experience it."

"And you admit that we make a good team?" he asked, although what she said about knowing that there was a fun person underneath his layers struck him a little. After all, he would have considered himself a fun person a long time ago, but not really anymore. He would have said that part of him was lost in the fire.

But maybe it wasn't lost, maybe he just buried it for a little bit.

"Of course. I'm the one who said it to begin with. And I never retracted it, just because you didn't agree with me didn't make it not true."

"Thank you for bringing out the fun part of me again." He appreciated the fact that she wasn't cowed by his ill humor and didn't give up on him when most people would want to run screaming away, because he wanted them to. Because he drove them to it.

"I think you're giving me more credit than I deserve again. After all, the fun part is there. Obviously. And you are allowing it to show for me, so maybe I ought to thank you."

He smiled, knowing she was deflecting his compliment, tossing it back to him, and he appreciated that humility. She wasn't arrogant and had never mentioned any of the accolades that she won as a reporter.

"If I ask a question, would you give me an honest answer?" he asked, figuring that the question probably wasn't necessary, but he wanted to make sure.

"Have I lied to you before?"

"No. Never. I just... Did you come here looking for a story?"

Her face clouded for just a moment, and he thought maybe he had offended her. He hadn't meant to.

But then, he could almost read the look on her face to say she deserved the question which wasn't really a fair assessment, and he wanted to argue with her, except she hadn't settled and she didn't give in. She lifted her chin.

"No. I did not come here looking for a story. It was exactly what I told you before, I came here a lot because my aunt lived here and I heard that you moved here. I wanted to meet you. I wanted to thank you. I wanted to know the person who saved my life."

"And?"

"You aren't what I thought you were going to be."

His heart sank.

"You're better. Better in so many ways. I guess in my thoughts and dreams you were a happy person, but you were just two-dimensional. I came here, and I met a man with a lot of layers, a lot of character, a lot of drive and compassion and patience and willpower. I... I felt you were so much more than what I was looking for."

They stared at each other for a bit, and he was tempted to put his hand on her cheek and move forward.

But she was a lot younger than he was; he was old and scarred, and she wasn't saying that she had found the man she wanted to be with, she was just saying she liked him. At least he thought that's what she was saying.

So he let his hands hang at his sides, until he remembered something they had talked about. Something about taking risks. Something about never finding out if he didn't step out.

"I wondered what became of you," he finally said softly.

"And?"

"And I guess I could say the same thing. I hadn't thought that you would become the woman you are. I guess in my head, you were always a fifteen-year-old girl. And now... You're a beautiful woman standing in front of me."

He felt a little uncomfortable in the silence that followed, but he also felt like he wanted to move forward. To take that risk.

"I think... I think God brought you to me at the exact right time. I needed you. And... I could see myself falling for a woman like you."

Maybe those weren't exactly the right words, but it was far more than he wanted to say. Far more than he was comfortable saying. Far more than he had ever told anyone else.

"A woman like me?" she asked, emphasizing the like. As though she had caught that maybe it wasn't her that he was going to fall for.

"I dread the next doctor's appointment. Not because people might see my face, but because when the doctor tells me that I can put weight on my leg and walk again, I know you will be leaving. I don't want that."

"Why?"

She seemed to be probing. Not letting him off the hook with just a few words of risk, but she wanted him to risk everything.

"Because I love being with you. I love seeing your smile, having you tease one out of me. Seeing the lines that form between your brows when you're concentrating at the table with your computer. Watching you try to cook. It's almost comical because you look at the recipe sixteen times, and then you still do the wrong thing."

She laughed. It was true.

"You're so kind, and whatever I need, you're there. You show up. And you love my horses. And you seem to like me okay."

"I definitely like you okay. I...like you more than okay."

Those words sent a charge down his fingers. He lifted a hand, running his fingertips down her cheek, easing the tingle that had settled there.

"How much is that?" he asked.

"I'm not sure," she said, and he could tell from the look in her eyes that her words were honest.

"Maybe we could work on finding out?" he asked, unsure what else to say. What else he could do that would keep her with him, help them explore whatever it was that he felt, and he could hardly believe it but she must feel at least a little bit too.

His heart thrilled when she nodded.

It stopped when she stepped forward and put a hand on his cheek.

It felt odd to have someone touching the scar, but she caressed it like he was whole and handsome and not shriveled and scarred.

"Does working on finding out how much we like each other involve anything else besides talking about Brussels sprouts and horses?"

"We can talk about football, but I probably wouldn't have very many interesting things to say."

"Just talking?" She lifted her brows.

He wasn't sure if she was saying exactly what he thought she was saying.

"So you think we can learn about each other without words?"

"Maybe not learn, but... I want to say I don't typically go into a relationship thinking that it's just a fling, but I don't typically go into relationships at all. So, I don't want to do this if you're not thinking about serious things."

He froze. Serious things? He had no idea what she was talking about there.

So he asked.

"I'm not sure what serious things are?"

"I think it's pointless to have a relationship if you're not looking to be married. You're just kind of wasting your time with someone; you're just in it for a good time. I know that that's kind of difficult today, and you can tell me I'm crazy if you want to, but that's how I feel. I...don't want to spend time getting to know someone and being close to them, and...falling for them, if there's no future."

She was talking about marrying him. She was talking about what they were doing, only with an eye toward marriage.

He almost swallowed his tongue. In fact, he kind of had to root around trying to find it. There it was, attached to the roof of his mouth and stuck there.

"I can't tell you the last time I thought about marriage. But it feels natural. Feels right. And... I think I'd like to kiss you."

# Chapter 20

He wanted to kiss her?

Eliza leaned closer. That wasn't exactly what she'd come here for all those weeks ago, but it had become something she'd wanted for a while; she couldn't even say how long.

She could hardly believe it was happening.

Her heart thumped, racing away in her chest, and her mouth felt dry, but she lifted her head anyway.

"Maybe it's better to wait, though," Hines said, and she barely stifled a groan of frustration.

"You shouldn't tease people like that," she said, and her voice was shaky.

His lips quirked just a bit, but he shook his head. "I wasn't teasing. I just think that you're right. We should make sure that we're serious about each other and that our relationship is headed in the right direction. Kissing isn't something that you should do with just anyone."

She agreed. She so agreed with that, but she didn't want to think that right now. She wanted to kiss and think later.

He was right.

She cupped his cheek, holding it for just a moment more, wanting to explore the way it felt, but not wanting to point out to him that it didn't feel the way she expected it to. Even though she had scarred legs that were just as scarred as his face, it was still different.

Regardless, if things worked out, there would be plenty of kissing later.

And if things didn't work out, she wouldn't regret not kissing tonight.

She appreciated his wisdom in knowing that. Not just knowing, but following through with his words and actions. Because she would have happily kissed him, if he would have allowed.

"I guess we're ready to see the horses?" she asked, knowing her voice wasn't nearly back to normal.

"Yeah. The horses would like to see us."

"That might be a little bit too positive for me."

"As long as we have food, they'll like to see us." He amended his statement, and she laughed.

She opened the door, and they went out together. She loved that he made her laugh. And she appreciated that he had said that he had had a good time at supper too. So maybe she made him laugh as well.

She felt like laughter healed the soul and kept a person young.

That was just her opinion, but she seemed to notice that the older people got, the less they seemed to laugh. So it had to be something that a person had to make a conscious choice about. That they were going to have fun. That they were going to enjoy life, that they were going to laugh.

"So you said that I made you laugh. And I was just thinking that laughter is a choice, happiness is something we decide to be. So it's not really me. It's you deciding that you're not going to keep your guard up anymore, but you're going to enjoy life. Right?"

He walked alongside her, his crutches thumping rhythmically on the frozen ground. "I think sometimes I know that life is a choice. I also think that sometimes we come across someone who unlocks pieces of our heart. Or that was a little sappy. I don't usually talk like that."

"You talk like that all the time. You were really waxing eloquent about Brussels sprouts this evening."

"That was not eloquent, that was...amazed that I was even getting them in my mouth and down my throat."

"Like I said. Eloquent."

He rolled his eyes but laughed as he continued to walk. "So maybe not have the key to open your heart, exactly, but where they just turn light bulbs on in your head. Show you life in a way you hadn't seen it before; point you in a direction that you hadn't considered going. And yeah, sometimes instructions are fun. And that's kind of what you did for me. You weren't scared away, and you made me see things I hadn't seen before. And maybe I listened to you because you have the same scars that I do. Or maybe there was just a connection. You know?"

"Okay. I guess I can agree that someone can say something to you that totally means nothing to you and you don't listen, but then someone else comes along and they say the same thing to you and it clicks in a way that nothing else ever has and just turns your whole world completely around so that you're looking at everything from a different angle that is new and better and shows you things you hadn't seen before."

"Exactly. I couldn't have said it better myself."

They had made it to the barn door, and he reached out, using his hand to slide it open.

That was one of those things that she wanted to do for him. She didn't want to see him struggle to open the door, brace himself against his crutch, and almost lose his balance. But she felt like it was something he wanted to do. That he wouldn't be happy if she were doing it for him.

So, she murmured thank you as she walked into the dim interior, going immediately to where the feed was kept, without needing the lights.

There were some scurrying sounds, and she almost wished she had turned the lights on.

"Do you think there's mice in the barn?" she asked, trying not to sound afraid.

"I can almost guarantee you there are mice in the barn. I hope there are no rats, but I can't say for sure there aren't."

"Are you serious? Mice are bad enough, but rats?"

"They're looking for a warm place to spend the winter too," he said simply. "If I were alone, I might spend some evenings out here with my .22 and a dim light. Dim enough that I can see but not bright enough that it will keep them from coming out, and I'd shoot them."

She didn't like that idea any better than she liked the idea that they were in here, but she knew sometimes you had to do hard things in order to protect what was yours.

"Do they eat a lot of feed?"

"They can't get into the garbage cans where we keep it, but they can gnaw through the feed bags if they put their minds to it, and they definitely get into the troughs and buckets if the horses don't eat the grain right away."

"I see. You don't have any cats?"

"I had one for a while, but about two winters ago, he disappeared for a while, and before I knew it, the winter was over and I realized I hadn't seen him for months."

"I had a friend in high school who said people kept dropping cats off at their barn, thinking that they had food or something. They had more cats than they knew what to do with. They tried to get them fixed, but they just kept breeding too fast. The cats ended up being more of a problem than the mice."

"I think that's probably a problem a lot of farms have. I've never had anyone drop them off here, but when people want to get rid of their animals, they often go to a remote place and drop them. It certainly isn't unheard of, and while sad, it's true."

She reached into the bag of feed, grabbing several handfuls of grain and shoving them in her pockets. "I'm putting some in my pockets for you, just so you know."

"I figured you'd take care of me," he said easily from over by the door. She supposed he didn't want to use his crutches in the dark, since the barn was a lot more cluttered than the yard.

Whatever it was, he didn't come over but closed the door behind her after she walked out.

She murmured thank you, and they walked in silence over to the paddock where Sassy had been staying since Miller had brought her five weeks ago.

They stopped at the edge of the fence, with Hines leaning his knee against the top of one of the slats, while Eliza put both of her forearms on the top one.

Sassy was clear over on the other side, and she snorted softly as they stopped.

"She's used to us feeding her over here, so she might walk over on her own."

"She's never come the whole way over before I got out of the paddock."

"I've noticed that. Which is typical. Whatever abuse she suffered, she is leery of people and doesn't want to be any closer to them than what she has to be."

"Do you think she'll ever tame down?"

"Yeah. I wouldn't have gotten her if I didn't think she was redeemable. I guess I kind of feel like all animals are redeemable. Although, Miller tells me I have a soft heart, and that might be the problem there."

Eliza laughed a little, but Hines had used the word redeem, and it made her think about the Lord and of how every person was redeemable. Sometimes it felt like there was no good in someone. Nothing worth saving, but Jesus saw something worth saving in everybody.

Interesting that Hines saw something worth saving in every horse.

She liked that contrast and smiled to herself.

"Hey, Sassy. Want to come on over here and get a little feed." She took a handful out of her pocket, cupped her hands together so she wouldn't drop any feed, and shook it so that the horse could hear she had something.

"If you give her a couple of moments, let the wind carry the smell of the feed to her, she might realize we've got something she wants, and maybe that'll inspire her to walk over."

"I've been trying to talk to her every time I feed her, just so she gets used to my voice."

"That's what I would do too. Just having conversations while you're feeding gets her used to hearing from us. Which is a good thing. Horses are smart. They know where their food comes from."

They stood and talked to her for a while, trying to get her to mosey over.

Eliza had to remind herself several times about what Hines had said about being patient and not expecting too much too soon. Because a person was sure to be disappointed.

After about ten minutes, they stopped talking to the horse and just talked with each other.

Hines said, "What are you planning on doing once I'm able to get around again?"

"I don't know. I had been looking for a job online so I could live in Sweet Water and work without having to travel. There are tons of jobs like that, but I was looking for something that would allow me to earn enough money to save and invest."

"Plans for the future?"

"Not really. I just...feel like it's the responsible thing to do, you know?"

"Yeah. I know what you mean. I guess, that's another thing about living here by myself. I've learned to be content with a lot less." He put a hand out. "I'm not lecturing you, just saying. When I lived in Texas, I felt like I needed money for a lot of things that I learned up here in North Dakota I didn't really need. Maybe that's one of the benefits of drawing away from people. You stop feeling pressure to conform. The need to have this or that or the other thing or people think you're weird."

"People already think I'm weird. I write everything down. I take notes about stuff."

"Not about anything important. Thinking of your inability to read a recipe and remember?"

"That has nothing to do with taking notes. Probably if I took notes on the recipe, I'd be able to follow it better."

"Maybe," he said, and his voice held a lot of disbelief.

"Actually, I do well when I have lists. Step one, step two, step three. Recipes are often all jumbled together."

"They just have too many things on the steps for you. Too much for your brain to remember."

"Something like that. I guess."

She had turned and was looking at him, the hand that was holding the grain forgotten as she leaned it on top of the board, gently cupping the feed in her palm.

"Don't look now. Don't move. But Sassy has walked over and her nose is about two feet away from your hand."

"You're kidding," she said, trying to keep her tone from holding any excitement or new notes in it. But it was hard not to show how excited she was that the horse had come over.

"She doesn't really look like she's going to keep moving, but she definitely wants to sniff your hand. Don't move."

"You think she's going to bite me?" Eliza asked.

Hines didn't laugh, but she had a feeling he was trying not to. "I guess you have gotten a couple of bites since you started feeding the horses."

"Three to be exact, and the third one was only because you told me not to worry, that horse doesn't bite." That was after she got bit by the first two and had been a little gun-shy.

Hines had told her that he would only let her feed the horses that he was sure would like her and not bite.

"All right. So you remember the lesson we learned from that."

"You're wrong," she said, trying not to shout it but say it in a voice that wouldn't scare Sassy. She still hadn't looked in that direction.

"No. Well, that's you, but we can never say for sure what a horse is going to do. And if you're going to work with horses, you're probably going to get hurt at some point. The only question is how much."

"So, we should be discussing whether I'm going to lose a finger or an entire arm?"

"Well, I had a broken arm for four weeks, and you took care of me, so I guess I should be able to take care of you if you lose yours."

"That was so reassuring. I just want you to know how much your words mean to me."

"Thank you. I try. It's not one of my fortes, but I've been told I've softened a bit over the past few weeks."

"You mean, you have someone arrive at your home and show you all the things you were missing in life, and make you want to leave the dark side and come over to the light."

"Is that what happened?" he said, sounding truly baffled. "My memory is a little fuzzy. I broke my leg and my arm, but they couldn't fix my brain."

"She's touching my hand," Eliza said, her voice a whisper, even though she meant to say it in the same tone she'd been using.

"I didn't want to scare you, but yeah. She took a step forward and looks like she wants what you're holding. You could probably carefully straighten your fingers out."

She did. So slowly. Like taking one finger at a time and stretching it out so that her hand was almost flat, just cupping it a little with the grain.

"She's sniffing. She's thinking pretty hard about it," Hines said.

"Do you think I can turn my head?" she asked, wanting to see so badly.

"If you turn it as slowly as you opened your hand, I think it will be okay."

So she did, agonizing over the slowness but being able to feel Sassy's breath on her hand, rushing across her fingers, and then the soft whiskers of her nose and the brush of her lips as she came out and nibbled the grain off.

"I can't believe it!" she said in a hushed whisper. "She's eating out of my hand!"

"I knew you could do it. I had all the faith in you."

"I didn't have all the faith in myself. I didn't think she liked me that much."

"Well. She likes grain that much anyway."

"You are so encouraging."

"I don't want you to get a big head. I like your humility."

"Thanks. I don't want a big head either. I guess I can't read in the Bible anywhere where anyone has ever been too humble. I suppose that is a character trait that I'll be able to work on until I die."

"I need to, too. And you're right. The world today kind of makes fun of people who are humble, and they would definitely say that a person could be too humble or too self-effacing, but the Bible doesn't indicate that at all. Definitely something we can all work toward."

That was true, and they lapsed into silence as Sassy ate the grain out of Eliza's hand and even came a little closer while they fed her the rest.

Looking back, Eliza couldn't imagine a better day.

# Chapter 21

"All right, with your new boot, you can start putting weight on your leg. I want you to keep it down to no more than four hours a day. Somewhere between two and four. We'll set up a video appointment for next week, we'll see how it's doing, and we might bump it up. But congratulations, you can walk again." The doctor smiled as he looked at Eliza's jubilant face.

Hines had to smile too. A person would have thought that Eliza was the one who was finally able to walk again.

After talking with her over the past week, he was pretty sure she wasn't happy because she wasn't going to have to come to his house anymore, but there was still that idea in his head. He hated that he was so insecure.

Gathering their things, they walked out a few moments later, him carrying his crutches.

"You had to get started right away, didn't you?" Eliza said, laughing at him gingerly walking on his leg.

"No better time than the present. Plus, it's already two o'clock in the afternoon. I only have a limited amount of time to get my four hours in today."

"Maybe it's not such a bright idea to start off with four hours. He said 'up to' four hours."

"So that means five or six if it really calls for it."

"You've already healed a lot faster than what they were expecting, you don't want to mess it up now."

He was just messing with her, and he was pretty sure she knew that.

As they turned the corner, his smile faded as the same woman and child that they'd seen the last time they were leaving came toward them down the hall.

They must have had a weekly appointment at the same time.

Neither one of them looked ill or had a cast or braces on. So Hines couldn't imagine what the issue was, and he really didn't care. All he wanted was to get away from the kid.

But then he told himself, no matter what he said, Hines was going to try to react with kindness.

The boy's eyes widened, and his mouth opened, then it closed. Then it opened again, and he lifted his head as he said, "Good day, sir."

Someone's mother had talked to him since the last time they'd seen him. Hines laughed to himself.

But his face remained serious as he nodded at the child and then said, "And good day to you, kind sir." His eyes were twinkling as he lifted them to meet the gaze of the mother. She had relief in hers, like she hadn't been sure whether her son was going to get the message or not and didn't know what he would say.

Hines figured if he had had a mother, she would probably have worn that expression a time or two.

He was still thinking about that after they made the appointment for the video call and a week later for another x-ray and walked out into the crisp North Dakota air.

"I think I'm going to see if I can contact my sister."

Eliza froze. He had to stop and look back at her.

"What?" he asked, like he had not just dropped the bombshell on her.

She gasped, a hand going to her chest like her heart could hardly contain itself.

He wasn't sure if he'd ever wanted to kiss anyone as much as he wanted to kiss her at that moment.

She knew what it meant to him, knew what the words meant, and was behind him a hundred percent.

He'd never had anyone in his life who supported him the way Eliza did. And she did it without seeming like she was supporting him. She definitely didn't make it seem like a drag or like something she had to do, but something that was...a privilege.

"I don't even know where she is now. If she's married, anything. But it is about time, past time, that I look around. I have so much apologizing to do to her too."

"That's beautiful," Eliza said, and when she started walking again, she moved forward, slipping her hand into his.

It surprised him for a moment, because while they'd done a lot of talking, and they'd worked together a good bit too, they hadn't walked around holding hands.

He liked it. Liked the feel of hers and his, liked the connection and the way it said that they were together. A couple. Belonging to each other maybe.

They didn't even talk that much on the way home. He just smiled, riding in the passenger seat and thinking about the day when they rode together forever. She had said that she didn't do relationships that were flings. So he knew that her slipping her hand into his was a serious thing for her.

He probably hadn't thought about things nearly as much as she had, but he had to agree with her. And could hardly contain the excitement and happiness he felt at the fact that everything in his life seemed to be falling into place.

Maybe it was because his outlook changed, and maybe it was a combination of that and the fact that God had brought the right person into his life, and she had stayed despite the fact that he had tried to drive her away.

They arrived home and were grabbing the few groceries that Eliza had grabbed at the store in Sweet Water out of the back of the car when an unfamiliar van drove up.

Hines tried not to allow himself to think that it seemed to be typical of his life, that as soon as something started to go well, something else dropped in to ruin everything. After all, he had no reason to suspect that the van was there for any reason other than a neighborly visit or a salesperson perhaps.

But still, he couldn't stop the ball of dread that formed in his chest, heavy and tight and hard.

"Do you recognize that vehicle?" Eliza asked as she came around the side of her car with two grocery bags in each hand and her purse over her shoulder.

"I don't. But I guess we'll find out who it is here in a minute," he said, his crutches tucked up underneath his arm and him carrying two grocery bags as well. He was happy to be back in the land of the living and the working, pulling his share. Or, if not his share, close to it.

He took the grocery bags inside and set them on the counter, then turned right back around and walked to the door, getting there just as a woman with a small young baby in a car carrier on one side of her and a young girl on the other had raised her hand to knock.

"I'm sorry. I wanted to put my groceries down before I came out to greet you. You can come in."

"Are you Hines Cannon?" the woman said, sounding rather formal.

"I am." He looked at the woman, then again at the children, and back to the woman.

"I have a message from your sister, Connie."

"Okay?" The ball that had been forming in his chest dropped into his stomach with a resounding thump.

"She said if anything ever happened to her, and she was unable to take care of her children, I was to bring them to you. We attended her funeral last week. This is Clara." She nodded at the little girl, then at the baby. "And this is Priscilla. If we didn't do something with these children, the state was going to get involved. I am grateful that the Internet has so much information and that I was able to find you. Are you going to be able to take the children?" she asked, rushing her words together as though she was afraid that he was going to slam the door in her face and she wouldn't be able to get all of the information out.

"Yeah. Of course." He didn't hesitate with his answer, but it wasn't as confident as what he wanted to be. In fact, he sounded bewildered. Which was fitting, since he felt bewildered.

"Connie passed away?" He narrowed his eyes, trying to get words out. How to say what he wanted to say? She was young. Younger than him. She shouldn't have died.

"Yeah. She donated a kidney over ten years ago to a stranger who happened to be a match. She didn't even know him. Then, she adopted Clara. She had a thing for special-needs children."

From the look on Clara's face, Hines guessed that she didn't like to be called special-needs. He didn't see anything wrong with her though. Of course, there didn't appear to be anything wrong with Eliza either.

"That's about the time she started having trouble with her other kidney. The remaining one. Then, she managed to get things under control, so she adopted Priscilla, who has a heart defect and is scheduled for surgery next week in Houston."

"Heart surgery in Houston?"

"Yes. And I guess the stress of dealing with all that was just too much for Connie's kidney, or maybe it was just going to go anyway. But whatever, she had been on dialysis since shortly after she adopted Priscilla. But she got an infection, and the end was fast."

"Okay." Wow. That was a lot. He had no idea. He had just been going to contact her, and the guilt was almost overwhelming. He hadn't known that she had so much on her plate and could have used his help. Why hadn't she contacted him?

Maybe because she couldn't find him. Maybe because she was afraid to. Maybe because she was mad that he had walked away the way he had.

He didn't know and probably would never find out.

"What hospital? What do I do?"

The lady held up her hand. "Don't worry about it. I have all of her medical information in a book. I also have the information that you will need in order to proceed with her care. Your sister named you as their guardian, and there's the paperwork we need to fill out, but you shouldn't have any trouble sliding into that role." The lady shrugged, looking a little annoyed. "North Dakota is a long way from Houston, so the care and coordination of it might be a little bit difficult, but perhaps you can have things moved to a hospital that's closer to you, or maybe you can move to Texas. The climate is certainly more hospitable down there."

The lady's southern drawl came out on that last bit, and Hines detected a touch of southern snobbery.

He laughed a little to himself, since he was a Southerner and a Texan, information this woman probably didn't know.

"How about you come in out of the cold. We can talk about this." Eliza had appeared at his elbow, and she spoke to the woman and children.

"I can't. I have some more things to carry in, clothes and such, and then I need to be off. I have a return flight that leaves Minneapolis in eight hours, and it's a six-hour drive there." She looked between Eliza and Hines. "Your sister didn't mention that you were married. That will make everything easier."

Hines opened his mouth, and he closed it again. The woman was leaving, and he probably would never see her again. There was no point in trying to correct anything.

Clara watched him with wide eyes though, and maybe he should have corrected things for her sake. It didn't matter, once they got her in, they would sit her down and get her story and give her theirs.

His day had just been completely turned on its head, and he was grateful for Eliza who stood beside him.

She didn't argue with the woman either but simply said, "I'll give you a hand carrying things in. Maybe we can talk about what exactly is going on as we do that."

"I told you everything I know, other than the backstories of the kids. I suppose I could tell you a little more about Connie, but the main thing about Connie is she was a one-of-a-kind woman. I've never met anyone more generous or giving than her. She would sacrifice herself to save someone else. And considering that she gave a stranger her kidney, which caused all her problems and her eventual death, she did."

Eliza nodded solemnly, and despite the lump of guilt that threatened to strangle him, Hines was proud of his sister. What beautiful words the stranger had for her. He appreciated them and loved knowing that his sister was such a wonderful woman.

He couldn't even process that his sister was no longer with him. He hadn't been able to say goodbye. He shoved those thoughts aside to deal with later.

Clara had stood stoically beside the woman, but as she turned to leave, she stepped back and glanced between the woman and Hines as though unsure whether she should step into the house or follow the woman back to the car.

The woman tossed over her shoulder, "You can carry the child in, Clara. Then you can get to know your uncle. He's going to take care of you from now on. He looks like a fine man, and I'm sure that your mom wouldn't have left you with him if he wasn't a good person."

With that, the woman walked down the walk, Eliza at her side, saying something, maybe asking a question, leaving Clara standing in front of Hines with Priscilla in the car seat, watching everything with wide eyes.

"Come on in, kiddo. I... I was just telling Eliza today that I wanted to get back in touch with your mom. I honestly couldn't be happier to see you on my doorstep right now. Except... I can't believe my sister's gone. I loved your mom."

Maybe it was that last sentence that melted Clara enough for her to pick up the baby carrier and step into the house.

Funny how life could sometimes change in a matter of moments. But it was clear to Hines that his would never be the same.

# Chapter 22

"Mom said you were a nice person and I would like you." The little girl spoke softly as Hines shut the door behind her and looked at these two strangers that were standing in his living room.

"You heard what the lady said about you."

"Miss Blue. That's her name."

"Miss Blue. You heard what Miss Blue said about you. That's all I know about you," he said, emphasizing the word "all." He couldn't believe his sister had children and she hadn't told him. He didn't know. He was an uncle.

"You don't look very happy." Clara looked up at him, then back down at the floor, like she wasn't sure whether that would make him mad or not.

"I'm shocked. I didn't know my sister had children. I'm an uncle. And I didn't even know. It makes me a little bit sad. It makes me even more sad that I'm never going to talk to my sister again." His voice got a little husky on that last phrase, and he stopped speaking for a moment. He didn't want to cry in front of these girls. But he had a lot of processing to do, the least of which was the processing of the death of his sister. How could she go without him getting a chance to say goodbye? The last things that he said to her was that he didn't want to embarrass her, and he didn't want to see her again, because being seen with him made her look just as bad as he did.

Man, if only he'd gone last week looking for her. He might have been able to at least say goodbye.

"Mom thought that you would love us. Because she said that you protected her when she was little."

"Yeah." He breathed out, trying to shove those memories aside, or he really would be crying. "I'm definitely gonna love you. Just because you're Connie's kids. But I think also because you're both amazing."

"We both have problems."

"That's okay. I have problems too. Obviously." They couldn't have missed his face, but Clara hadn't said anything, and Priscilla was too little to care. She sat in her car seat, chewing on her fist.

"You want to tell me about your problems?" he asked, hating it when people asked him, and thinking maybe he should start out talking about himself, to make her more comfortable talking about herself. "Hang on. Let me tell you about mine."

Before he could say anything, the door opened, and Miss Blue and Eliza came back in. Miss Blue was talking a mile a minute, rolling two large suitcases in the door, while Eliza had a bag slung over each shoulder, a suitcase in one hand, and a thick book full of what looked like papers jutting out everywhere in another.

"Everything you need to know is in that book. You can look things up online. The website to get all of the information is listed. Passwords are there as well. The name and number of the lawyer that she was dealing with is in there. Doctors, their names, numbers, hospitals, surgeries, including the planned surgery for next Tuesday."

Miss Blue tapped the cover of the book. "My number is on the cover there. You can call me if you need me. I hate to run out on you, but I don't have a choice. I didn't realize I was going to be driving so far from the airport. And I thought I would have plenty of time to sit around and chat. Unfortunately, I'm going to miss my flight if I don't get moving."

"That's fine. You go, I'm sure we will be in contact with any questions we have." Eliza lifted her brows at Hines who shrugged and nodded. He had no idea what to ask, since he had no idea what they were facing.

"You two be good. Clara, you take care of your little sister and answer any questions they have."

"Yes, ma'am," Clara said softly. But she didn't seem shy or retiring. She just seemed...sad. Which made sense. Her entire life had been upended.

Hines could relate. There had been multiple times in his childhood where his whole life had been upended. Where he'd ended up in a new house with a new set of parents and new rules and new everything. Things that were so hard to adjust to, things that scared him as he lay in bed at night. Wondering whether this was the time where he and Connie would finally be separated. Wondering why he couldn't have a normal family, parents who loved him, who wanted him and fought for him no matter what.

The door closed behind Miss Blue, and the room was quiet for a few moments. Even the baby's gurgling had quieted as though she too were thinking about the seriousness of the occasion.

"You were going to tell me what happened," Clara said, and her words were just as serious as they had been before.

"I was." Hines nodded, looking over at Eliza who jerked her head up, like she was fine with whatever he decided to do. So, he sat down right where he was in the middle of the living room floor, trying not to wince as his leg shifted oddly under him.

He'd completely forgotten about his broken leg and the boot that he was wearing.

Regardless, he settled himself on the floor, sitting in front of Clara.

Clara looked at him like he was crazy for all of three seconds, and then she settled herself on the floor beside him.

"I was a firefighter."

"Mom told us you were."

"There was a fire and explosion at the school, and there was someone trapped inside. No one else heard her crying for help, except me."

"Mom said you were very brave to go back inside."

"I just did what I knew needed to be done. I didn't think about being brave. I just thought about the job."

"Weren't you scared?"

"No. I wasn't scared until I got in there, and I saw her trapped underneath the burning beam, and she was on fire. I didn't realize until later that I was on fire too. I just knew I needed to get us out."

"Did she live?"

"I did," Eliza interrupted, coming over and sitting down not too close but close enough to make a bit of a circle.

"It was you?" Clara showed emotion for the first time. Surprise.

"Yes. It was me."

"Mom didn't tell me that you married her."

"Well..." Hines looked at Eliza. "I haven't married her yet."

"You're living together?" Clara asked, and there was clear disappointment in her voice.

"No."

"No."

They spoke together. Then Hines lifted his brows, and Eliza gave another nod, indicating he could go ahead.

"I didn't have any contact with Eliza after the fire either. She heard that I might be living in Sweet Water, and she came multiple times trying to find me. It wasn't until I broke my leg," he rapped his knuckles on the boot he was wearing, "and my arm, that she came and took care of me and told me who she was."

"But she didn't move in?" Clara asked.

"No. She's been here during the day, coming early in the morning and staying until late at night. It makes for a long day and is a lot of work for her, but I appreciated it, because with a broken arm and a broken leg, I couldn't do too much."

"Yeah," Clara said.

"So, we've been catching up, and... I found I really like her. A lot." His eyes went from Clara to Eliza. She was smiling softly at him. He looked her in the eyes as he spoke. "I would like to marry her if she would have me. But I haven't asked yet. It's only been six or seven weeks."

"Mom said sometimes it doesn't take very long for people to know that they love each other."

"Did your mom ever get married?"

"She married someone who needed help. That's what she said. She helped him until he died."

Hines had the feeling that Clara knew more than what she was saying, but he didn't push her. "What about you?"

"I'm missing a leg."

Hines stared at her. He hadn't noticed, either when she was sitting down or when she tucked her feet under her. But his eyes went to the little gap between the bottom of her pant leg and shoe, and he could see the metal prosthesis sticking out.

"I see that now. But I didn't notice until you said something."

"I've learned to be pretty good with it. And Mom said she got money from you and she didn't hesitate to use it to get me whatever I need, so she said this prosthesis is the best that money can buy."

That was Connie. He had to smile. She'd used his money to help people. He should have known that's what she would do with it. That's the kind of person she always was. Thinking about others.

"You have to look in the book to find out about Priscilla. I know she had a heart defect she was born with. Her parents abandoned her in the NICU, and Mom was her foster mom and was able to adopt her. But she said that you would end up raising her."

"She had so much faith in me. She didn't know how I've turned out."

"She knew better than anyone. She saw how good you are. And knew that there was no way that you could be anything but a good husband and father."

He turned his face up to look at Eliza. Connie wasn't the only one who believed in him. She had from the very beginning too.

"All right. So we'll have to read the book on Priscilla. In the meantime, she probably needs food. As do you."

Clara shrugged, like she didn't care whether she ate or not.

"How long were you with your mom?" Hines asked.

"Since I was little. My leg had to be amputated shortly after birth. It was deformed when I was born, and there was some kind of infection in it before I turned one."

"I see."

"How old are you?" Eliza asked.

"I'm ten."

That surprised Hines. He figured that Connie must have adopted her shortly after the fire and he moved.

She was probably looking for an opportunity to use her money for good.

They spent the next couple of hours emptying the suitcases, getting the rooms ready for the girls, and eventually Eliza warmed up a meal that Alice had left and they all sat at the table eating.

It was a late evening, and the girls seemed tired. So, Priscilla went to sleep in her pack and play, after they gave her the blood pressure medicine she was supposed to have, along with several other medications she had been prescribed to help with the issues she had.

Hines was so grateful for Eliza's help, because he felt more than a little overwhelmed. He couldn't have kept the medication straight, got the girls ready for bed, fed them, unpacked, and figured out how they were sleeping.

Thankfully, he had an air mattress that he had used when he first moved and had packed away. Eliza found it, and it made a good enough bed for Clara for the time being.

Obviously they were going to have to adjust. All of them.

It was almost nine o'clock by the time they tiptoed out of the girls' rooms, turning out the lights and walking into the dining room.

"That was not the way I saw today turning out," he said as they stood in the living room facing each other.

"You should probably sit down and take the weight off that leg. I'm pretty sure you exceeded your four-hour limit."

"Always looking out for me," he murmured as he sat down obediently.

He certainly wasn't going to argue about that. She was right. He'd been on it far more than he should have been.

"And I agree. This is not something I had envisioned either."

She sat down in the chair facing him, on the edge of it, as though she couldn't settle herself.

He reached over and put a hand on her knee. She smiled at him and then covered his hand with hers. He rolled his hand, threading their fingers together.

They didn't say anything, just looked at their hands for a minute until he said, "Thank you so much for being here. There was just no way I was going to be able to get all that done."

"There was no way I could walk out when I knew you needed help."

"Is that the only reason you stayed?"

"I think you know it's not."

"Maybe I needed to hear it."

"I stayed because I'm hoping that someday those children will be mine too." She let out a breath. "And I stayed because I couldn't walk away from someone who needed me. Especially when I care for them as much as I care for you."

Leave it to Eliza to be brave. He squeezed her hand.

"I just...can't believe that Connie is gone. But I can't even process that because I can't believe that there are two lives in there that are depending on me. Someone that's scheduled for heart surgery next week. I feel like...it's more than I can handle."

"It's not more than you can handle. We're doing it together."

"The doctor just gave me permission to walk on my foot today. You don't need to be here anymore." His eyes searched hers, his breathing shallow. This wasn't how he expected them to say good-bye. And yeah, she said she would be here to help, but was she going to continue to come? How often? When?

"Maybe we need to talk about that."

"We do?"

"Yeah. I'm here for you. What do you want from me?"

"Everything." That wasn't a hard question.

"Done." She answered readily as well. It was not a hard answer for her apparently.

"You can't do that. Look at how my life has just been totally rearranged. I've got horses that need me, kids, a leg that's barely healed—"

"And someone right here who is going to help you with it all. Relax. We also have God. He's here for both of us."

"I can't expect you to help. You have no obligation to me."

"Maybe it's time that changed." Eliza's words were sincere, and her eyes drilled into his.

It took a minute for him to understand what she was saying. "You want to get married?"

"That would change things, wouldn't it? Then I would have an obligation. Then you'd stop wondering whether I was going to be beside you or not. I'm here. I told you that. But I get it. I don't have any responsibility. Not yet."

"And you'd marry me?" He couldn't help it. She had totally floored him.

"You sound like you don't want to. Don't feel like you have to."

"No. That's not it. I'm just shocked that could even be a solution. But I love it."

"Good."

While that scared him on one level, it calmed all his anxieties on another. If Eliza was truly with him, as his wife, he didn't have anything he needed to be afraid of. He had the Lord and Eliza, and between the three of them, of course they could handle it all.

"God knew I was going to need you, because he knew that the girls were coming, because he knew that I'm going to have to somehow fly to Houston and take Priscilla to her surgery."

"We probably ought to enroll Clara in school and get her going on that as quickly as possible as well. We don't want her to fall behind."

"True. So we need someone here, someone in Houston, and... Are you sure about this?"

"I'm sure. And whatever happens in Houston, maybe you could explain to the doctors that you live in North Dakota and perhaps all of her follow-up care can be done here. I haven't read the book yet. I don't even know what her surgery is for."

"Me either. Maybe... Maybe we should do that now."

"And maybe we had enough excitement for one day. It probably won't hurt you to let it go until tomorrow. Maybe we can enroll Clara in school, figure out what the girls need, and go from there."

"You'll come at your regular time?"

"Yes. At my regular time."

She stood, and he struggled to stand too. His leg ached. It wasn't the sharp pain of the original break, but the pain of muscles that were not used to being used.

"I think I'll take a kiss."

"Now that I asked you to marry me?"

"I'm pretty sure that was me asking you."

"I don't think so. I mean, we can argue about it if you want to, but I'm pretty sure it was my idea."

"All right. You win," he murmured as he moved closer, putting a hand around her waist and another one around the back of her head, burying his fingers in her hair.

She stepped closer without hesitation, looking up at him and smiling. There was no question in his mind that she wanted to be near him. And from the look in her eyes, he was pretty sure there were some strong emotions there.

"We'll get through this together," she said, her smile reassuring.

"As long as you're with me, together we can do it. And I'm going to be sure to thank the Lord for sending you. He knew just what I needed."

"And me."

She lifted her head as he lowered his, and he kissed her, and the worries about tomorrow, and the events of that day, and the craziness of the evening all faded away as he pulled her closer, and deepened the kiss, and wished that she wasn't leaving.

But tomorrow was another day, and it lightened his heart beyond words that they would face it together.

# Chapter 23

Eliza walked softly into the kitchen in the early, predawn light. "I heard there are some exciting things that happened at Hines's farm yesterday," Aunt April said from the table where she sat.

"My goodness. Where in the world did you hear that?" She couldn't understand where her aunt got her information. It had been late when Eliza had come home, and her aunt had already been in bed.

"Well, Miss Blue stopped at the diner on her way back through, wanting to grab some of the famous Marry Me Chicken. She talked to Jane, who talked to Miss Helen, who called me this morning and talked with me. But I wanted to hear from you."

"Well, it's true. There were a lot of things that happened."

"Did his sister die?"

"Yes," Eliza said, and then she went into a brief rundown of everything.

Everything except her impending marriage. She didn't know when or where or how or anything about it, and she didn't know what she would say to Aunt April. So she didn't say anything.

But as her aunt was digesting everything that she had said, she realized that she didn't know when she was getting married. Probably it wouldn't be today, but... It could be.

She cleared her throat and then looked at the floor. "I, well, you know that Hines and I have been getting kind of close."

Actually, she had downplayed any part of their relationship that hinted at romance, so this was going to be a bit of a shock to her aunt.

"I've heard you say he's a good man," Aunt April said. She looked at her Bible, running a loving hand over the page, flattening it, before she said, "The days I stayed with him, I have to admit I was surprised. I wasn't expecting to like him as much as I did. A recluse has a certain type of reputation even if it's not deserved."

That was true. She had certain thoughts about the way Hines was going to be before she actually met him.

"But he talked really well about you. He praised you and said how much he appreciated you helping him. I know I probably didn't say a whole lot about that because I don't think he wanted me to. I don't think he wanted you to know necessarily, he just wanted me to know how much he respected and liked you. I appreciated that about him. He wasn't trying to get any brownie points with anyone, he just wanted me to know what a wonderful woman you were." Her aunt laughed. "I told him I already knew, and that's why I had you here in Sweet Water. Because I wanted to find you a man who deserved you."

"Aunt April, that's really sweet of you, but I don't deserve that. I'm not any better than anyone else."

"You're my niece. And that makes me want the very, very best for you."

She couldn't argue with that, and she appreciated her aunt showing her love in that way.

"We decided yesterday that we were going to get married."

There. She said it.

Her aunt's expression didn't change. Her smile, if anything, grew bigger. "That's fantastic. I honestly hoped that would happen all along. So many years ago when he rescued you, it wasn't exactly romantic, because you were both hurt really bad, but it was in the back of my mind that the two of you might end up together after you came here to Sweet Water. I don't know, maybe I'm just a romantic."

"It wasn't you that sent Billy out to his ranch?" Eliza asked with her eyes narrowed. Everyone said he was a matchmaking steer, but she wondered if Billy wasn't being controlled by a mastermind because cows weren't exactly known for their ability to think.

"I wish I could take credit for it. But Billy has me beat hands down when it comes to matchmaking. But I couldn't let Billy one-up me with my own niece, now could I?"

"Well, I guess it was you and Billy together, since Billy's been out at Hines's ranch since I got there. I kind of wonder if we get married whether he'll leave." That had been something that had been bouncing around in her head. If Billy truly was a matchmaking steer, surely once his work was done, he would be on to someone else.

"Of course, when he matched Kenni, she got a pig out of the deal. I haven't gotten anything."

"Billy made sure you got a horse."

Eliza didn't argue with her aunt, but it wasn't quite the same thing.

"You know if you need any help with the children, I'll help you out however I can."

"I know that. I have to talk to Hines about it today. I'm thinking that it might be best for Clara to just settle down in school and start making friends. But we'll see what Hines says. He might want everyone to go to Houston for Priscilla's surgery."

"The sisters might be close. Maybe they'll want to stay together."

"Priscilla's too little to say. I forget exactly how old she is, but it's less than a year. And Clara seems rather protective of her, but I don't know that they bonded that much if you know what I mean."

"I understand. Not like two sisters who are talking and sharing secrets and so on. Priscilla I'm sure knows Clara, recognizes her and feels safe with her, but it's not like they've known each other for years and have depended on each other to get them through the hard times."

That was exactly what Eliza meant.

"At any rate. If you need me, you know you can call me. And I really think that everything is going to work out. I have a good feeling about it. And I've been praying for you."

Eliza went over, hugging her aunt. It was always good to know that there was someone behind her praying. It...made her day go better.

Gave her a more positive outlook. There was something to be said about prayer and the way it changed a person's mind and thoughts to know that people cared enough to whisper their name before the Father.

She did a little praying herself on the drive out to Hines's house.

It surprised her that she wasn't praying more for herself. She just agreed yesterday to marry someone she'd only known for six weeks. But she wasn't worried about that at all. In fact, she was looking forward to that.

Sure, there was a little bit of nervousness there, but it was an anticipatory type of nervousness. Not a fear that she was making a big mistake. She had no doubt she was making a good decision. Her prayers were more for the girls. For Clara and Priscilla, having lost their mom, having had such a rough start in life. Having so much instability around them.

And yet, as she prayed, she was reassured because Hines had had that same instability. He knew, maybe not exactly what they were going through, but very close. And she had every confidence that he would do everything in his power to let the girls know that they were going to be putting down roots. That they'd made their final move. Until they graduated and chose to move out of their home.

She liked the idea that they were making a stable home for two girls who needed it. And she loved that Hines was willing to come out of his shell to do that.

In fact, he hadn't mentioned one time yesterday anything about the girls being ashamed of a father who looked the way he did.

Maybe he was coming to grips with that. Accepting what had happened to him, and the way he looked, and determining to make the best of it. Maybe losing his sister because he had walked away from her, losing her without saying goodbye or anything, had shown him that pulling himself away from people didn't help anyone and only hurt them.

She could only hope anyway.

She usually rapped on the door before she walked in, but she could hear Priscilla crying before she even opened it.

Hines looked relieved to see her as she closed the door behind her, holding the baby in a gingerly way that clearly said that this was like the second time in his life that he ever held a baby before and the first time he held one that was inconsolably crying.

Eliza didn't have any more experience than what he did, but she walked over anyway.

"Did you try feeding her?" That seemed to be the first answer that anyone gave when a baby was crying.

"She spit the bottle out. Clara said that's the way she acts when she isn't hungry."

"Burp?" Eliza asked, although she thought it was little babies who needed to be burped. Not babies who were old enough to sit up, which was Priscilla's age.

"Clara said she didn't need to be burped anymore."

"Maybe she's missing her mom?"

Hines nodded. "That's kind of the conclusion I came to, but I'm worried because she's crying so hard. Surely that's not good for her heart? I didn't get a chance to look through the material, and I don't know if it is okay to just allow her to cry, or if I need to give her some kind of sedative to calm her down..."

"Clara?" Eliza asked the little girl who was still sitting at the breakfast table, a clean, empty plate in front of her.

"I think it's okay. Sometimes she cried for Mom. Although, Mom was really good at getting her to stop. She said I was fussy when I was a baby, and she got lots of practice with me."

"All right. Well then, I guess we'll get our practice. Maybe I'll grab the book and see if I can see whether it says whether or not she's allowed to cry, okay?"

Hines nodded, still bouncing the baby, and she looked at his foot. He was on it already today. And still only supposed to be on it for four hours.

But now wasn't the time to remind him that he probably should be sitting down. How could someone sit down when they had a baby that was crying and they needed to try to get her to stop?

But as she was walking over to grab the book that Hines had set on the table, she wondered if maybe Priscilla was used to women? After all, Connie wasn't married, and Priscilla didn't have a father, and maybe she associated men with doctors and pain.

She walked back over. "I don't have any experience with babies at all, not even a little bit. I didn't even babysit when I was growing up, but maybe Priscilla just wants a woman?"

Hines looked relieved to hand her over, and Eliza had to admit she was relieved when Priscilla stopped crying almost immediately.

"You might be onto something there," Hines said, and Priscilla's watery eyes turned to him, listening to his deep voice.

"Well, I didn't really want to be, not that I don't want to hold the baby, but I liked it when you have that responsibility. This makes me nervous," Eliza said with a smile.

"Well, you're good at it. If that's any consolation."

"It is. A little."

"I talked to Clara a little bit before Priscilla woke up, and she'd like to be enrolled in school today. She wants to go meet some new friends and get started settling in."

"All right. That sounds good." She didn't know whether he would want her to stay home with the baby or go with them. But then with his next words, her heart leapt.

"I thought you and I could go on to Rockerton and stop at the courthouse."

"...And get married?" she asked, trying not to gulp.

"Get a license at least. If we can get the pastor to marry us, I'd prefer that."

"Me too."

"Then we'll have that settled. Not that I want to get it out of the way, just..."

"I get it." She didn't need him to do all the romantic things when his life was in such a crazy chaos. Maybe it wasn't wise for them to step into marriage when there was so much unsettled around them, but it felt like the right thing to do. She felt a total peace about it, and she was guessing he did too.

"Then, we'll have to figure out how we're going to handle the surgery on Tuesday. It starts at six o'clock in the morning, and they want her to be admitted to the hospital sometime Monday afternoon. So she's there in the NICU for them to prep her. So that means I'll either need to fly out Sunday night or Monday morning. Me, you, Clara, or some combination of us."

"All right. We have some decisions to make and things to do, but it sounds like we have things organized and at least know what we need to make decisions about, which is nice." She appreciated the fact that he was trying to make some order out of the chaos.

"I don't want to go to Houston. The drive is long, the plane ride is long, and it's boring sitting at the hospital waiting for them to be done with the surgery. And I just get scared that she's going to die and not come out. I'd rather be in school." Clara spoke up from the table.

"That's fine with me. Then we'll just figure out who's gonna take her to the surgery and who's gonna stay here with Clara."

"All right. We can talk about that later. Right now, if you don't mind, I'm going to cook Clara some breakfast. She needs some food in her belly so that she can go to school and learn all the things."

While Hines cooked breakfast, and again when he and Clara went out to feed, Eliza familiarized herself with the book that had all of Priscilla's medical information in it. There was a lot to read. But it looked like Tuesday could possibly be the last surgery. Although the recovery time was anything from four to ten days. And if the surgery didn't go well, there could be an additional surgery.

For the sake of their family, Eliza hoped it didn't take that long.

When Hines and Clara came back in, Hines was smiling. "I'm pretty sure Billy was very satisfied with himself this morning. At least, I think he looks smug. That's the word we used, smug?" He looked at Clara, as if clarifying that he had the right word.

"That's what you said. I agree. Although, that was really my first time to be close to any cow."

"Steer. Billy will be very offended if you call him a cow." Eliza lifted her brows at Clara.

They had plenty of time to get to school, which was one of the benefits of getting up early, and Eliza sat in the car with Priscilla while Hines took Clara in and filled out the paperwork for the school.

Clara was practically walking on air as she went in, eager to make friends and get to know the people in her new home.

She couldn't wipe the smile off her face.

Even though there was a lingering sadness lurking around her eyes. It hadn't been that long ago that she lost her mother. But everyone said children were resilient, and Eliza had to say that Clara definitely seemed that way.

On the way to the courthouse, they talked a little about taking Priscilla to her surgery, and Hines said that he thought it should be him.

"Are you sure?" Eliza asked, not wanting him to step out of his comfort zone too far too fast.

He'd gone from never getting out to getting out every few weeks for his doctor's appointment to...flying with a young child and going into the hospital and dealing with her major heart surgery?

"Yeah. I think that that should be me. Even though she's better when she's with you, I just feel like this is something I should do." He paused for a moment. "I wanted to see Connie's grave too."

Eliza could totally understand, and she nodded. "I'm fine with whatever you want to do. I honestly am happier staying home, and Clara seems like such a fine kid, I'm really excited to spend some time with her and get to know her."

"She did seem really happy this morning, didn't she?"

They had some issues to take care of at the courthouse, some questions that needed to be answered with the paperwork regarding custody of the children and the different things that they needed to do. They were shown to the right areas, and then before they left, they picked up a marriage certificate.

"Are you sure about this?" Hines asked, waving the piece of paper in the air as they walked down the steps of the courthouse. He had Priscilla in his other hand, and she'd been good all morning, content in her car seat, cooing and falling asleep on the drive to Rockerton.

"That's the one thing I'm really not the slightest bit nervous about."

"I can't offer you a spare room."

"I know. And... I'm okay with that if you are."

"I'm definitely okay. I wanted to make sure you were. That's a big step."

"And like I said, it's the one I'm not worried about."

The pastor had said he would be at the church in Sweet Water and would marry them whenever they got there. Eliza had called her Aunt April, and Hines had Miller standing up for him. They were all waiting at the church when they pulled up.

Hines shook Miller's hand while Aunt April put her hand on her chest and came forward with her arm out to hug Eliza.

Priscilla sucked on her fist and watched the goings-on with wide eyes.

The pastor said, "We can walk to the front of the church. I usually conduct the ceremonies there." They walked up the aisle, and the pastor continued, "Usually I have a time for marriage counseling beforehand. Just a few words that I like to say to the couple to remind them that this is a big step. Do you have time?"

Eliza nodded. Although she was a little concerned because Hines had spent so much time on his leg, but she thought that they both wanted their marriage to be as good as it could be.

As they settled down, the Pastor opened his Bible and said, "Marriage is a sacred covenant between a man and woman. It symbolizes the union between Christ and the church. It is a sacrament that is meant to be for life. That is one of the things that it symbolizes. The union between Christ and the church is permanent. God meant for the union between a man and his wife to be permanent. It is not a covenant that is to be broken. God hates divorce. He hates divorce because the union that marriage symbolizes is not ever to be broken."

He paused a moment and looked up, then continued. "The husband, as the head of the wife, is to lay down his life for his wife, the way Christ laid down his life for the church. The wife is to be submissive to the husband and obedient, the same way the church is to be submissive and obedient to Christ. I know that does not fly in our ungodly, unchristian, secular society, but it is Bible. The Bible says in Ephesians, **For the husband is the head of the wife, even as Christ is the head of the church: and he is**

**the saviour of the body.** In that same passage it also says, **Wives, submit yourselves unto your own husbands, as unto the Lord.**"

Another pause as he gazed steadily at them, letting the words sink in. "As Christians, we want to follow the world. We get upset when people try to tell us that we're not doing things correctly, and we use the world to justify ourselves. But God was not wrong. He knew exactly what we needed, what would be best for us. What would be best for our children. A permanent union between a wife, who was submissive and obedient, and a husband, who loves his wife and gives himself for her. When a husband loves his wife like that, submission and obedience is easy for the woman. Because she knows her husband will do anything for her. To the point of giving his life for her. The husband, when he has a submissive, obedient wife, knows he has found a rare jewel, and he will do anything for her."

Eliza nodded, seeing Hines doing the same from the corner of her eye. Everything the pastor was saying fit with her own understanding of the Lord's words. But she didn't say anything, for the pastor hadn't finished speaking.

"That picture that it paints to the world, when people look on a Christian marriage and see a husband who will give his life for his wife, who is loving and benevolent, and the wife who reverences her husband, they see that picture, and it can't help but point them to Christ and the picture of what he did for the church. We take that beautiful, holy picture, and we've reduced it to a sitcom. A punch line. A laugh track. Something that's a throwaway idea. We don't even bother to get married anymore, we just move in together. And it cheapens the relationship. It affects the vows we make and the decisions that we decide on. We forget that it's a holy sacrament. Holy as in something that God considers important and sinless. If we want to please the Lord, we need to consider the things holy that He considered holy. And not take a light view of our marriage. Once those vows are said, they are for life."

The pastor paused again, then took a breath. "And remember, your marriage is a picture of the relationship between Christ and the church. Think about that on a daily basis when you are tempted to be irritated with your spouse. Would the church be irritated with Christ? Of course not. Would Christ be irritated with the church? No. You never know who might be listening and watching you, looking at you to base their marriage on or to bring them to the Lord. Let them see through your marriage that there is such a thing as grace and love and forgiveness and that those things can be given freely, without restraint. And when two people in a marriage both give those things, they create a relationship that is beautiful and holy and sacred."

He shut his Bible, then smiled a little. "Now, I assume that my little speech has not changed either one of your minds?"

Eliza shook her head, and Hines said, "No. It was inspiring."

Eliza smiled. She had found it inspiring as well. She wanted to get started doing the hard work. Although she figured there would be times where she was frustrated and uneasy, as long as Hines was working as hard as she was, and even if he wasn't, she would continue to do her best, but if he worked as well, there was no way that they couldn't stay married for the rest of their lives.

The marriage ceremony was over before they knew it, and Hines leaned down, brushing her lips with his, as Aunt April and Miller clapped behind them.

It might not have been the wedding she thought she might have, but it was a beautiful wedding nonetheless, because she knew without a shadow of doubt that she loved the man beside her and would spend the rest of her life supporting him and loving him and doing everything she could to make his life better.

# Chapter 24

I t had been a beautiful wedding. The best. As they walked toward their car, Eliza couldn't stop smiling. But then, she realized that they hadn't heard anything out of Priscilla since before the pastor started his marriage counseling.

"Has Priscilla been sleeping all this time?" There was a little bit more panic in her voice than what she meant there to be. After all, she hadn't been doing this mother thing for very long. And she wasn't sure how long kids slept during the day and whether it was normal for them to sleep through so much chaos.

Although, Priscilla had an issue, and Eliza remembered reading there were things they needed to watch for. If anything of those things happened, they were to take her to the ER immediately.

One was a temperature.

One was fast, shallow breathing. She wracked her brain to think of any more.

Hines had stopped, and they both looked down at the baby in the car seat.

Her eyes were closed, and she seemed to be sleeping peacefully, except her cheeks were red, and her chest moved up and down in what Eliza thought was maybe a little faster than normal? She wasn't sure.

"Do you think she's okay?" she asked, reaching down and putting a finger on her forehead.

She was bundled up for the North Dakota cold, so maybe she had gotten a little warm in the church.

But there was no sweat. She felt hot and dry.

"I think... I think she needs to go to the ER."

"I feel like the worst father in the world. I never even thought. I was just happy she was sleeping through everything."

"Me too. I... I just was thinking that maybe it was a little odd that she slept through so much. But I don't know."

While they were talking, they had started walking as fast as they could to Eliza's car.

Hines was noticeably limping on his foot. And again, she thought he was on it too much but didn't say anything.

"I'll start driving toward the ER. Do you mind looking up the doctor's number and calling him? Asking him what we should do? We're so far away from her normal doctors."

Hines nodded abruptly as he yanked open the door and buckled Priscilla's car seat.

That would be terrible if they lost their daughter because they hadn't checked her enough. Why had they been complacent?

Why hadn't she checked her every half an hour, just checking?

She was beating herself up, and she knew she needed to stop. She was new, and normal parents make mistakes. Let alone someone who had not dreamed of having children yesterday and today had two.

Glancing at the dash, wondering if she would have time to drop Hines off at the ER in Rockerton and drive back to pick up Clara at school, she figured that if nothing got in her way, it should be okay.

She listened intently as Hines had a terse conversation with the doctor. Most of his words were yes and no after he explained what happened.

He even used the video chat for a few seconds, showing the doctor what she looked like.

"All right. We'll do it," he said, and then he hung up. "We're to take her to the ER. Let the doctors there get her stabilized, and then the doctor wants us to fly down there as soon as possible. A medical flight if necessary. He thinks that she's going into congestive heart failure and needs her surgery sooner rather than later."

"The fever?" She always thought fever indicated infection.

"He wasn't entirely sure. But he said they would look at her when she got down there. He wanted it to be as soon as possible. He's calling the ER in Rockerton and giving them some instructions and then going to leave his number."

"I can't believe you were able to get a hold of him."

"He knew all about Connie. Apparently she was a special favorite, and as soon as I mentioned her name, it was like his antenna went out and he was all ears. I owe a lot to my sister."

"For sure, if that's the way the doctors treat us when we mention her name."

They didn't talk much the rest of the way into Rockerton. Maybe Hines was beating himself up as much as she was. But she still had to be amazed that Hines was stepping out the way he was. She didn't want to point it out to him, but she definitely wanted to talk about it later. Maybe it was because of his sister that he seemed to have conquered all of his issues.

She hoped it was a permanent thing.

She pulled into the ER, right next to the door.

"I can't stay. I need to get back in order to pick up Clara at school."

"I know. And that's fine. We could have gotten someone else, but I think it's best for you to do it. Thank you for being willing." He leaned across the console, and she leaned toward him, and he gave her a quick kiss. He shook his head as he leaned back. "This was not what I anticipated for our wedding day. Sorry."

"It's okay, just take care of yourself, take care of Priscilla."

"I'll call Miller and have him bring some clothes down. You'll probably pass him on the way. I hope he gets here before they fly us wherever they're going to fly us."

"I hope they'll take you to Texas. I can just see this being something the insurance will decline."

"If it's better for her to have the surgery here, then I think that's what we need to do. The doctor had mentioned something about that, the flight being long, and it being difficult to secure one at this late date. Regardless, whatever happens happens."

"Yeah. It's probably best for us just to be prepared for anything."

She thought maybe she should be prepared for Priscilla's death. That would be included in everything.

But her mind shoved the thought away. She didn't want to think about losing the little girl whom she'd only known for twenty-four hours but already loved so deeply. She couldn't believe the panic that was rushing through her at the thought of anything happening to her.

She prayed the whole way back to the school and then gave Clara the watered-down version of what was happening.

She told her the truth, just tried to do it in a cheerful tone that hopefully gave Clara the idea that she wasn't completely petrified they weren't going to be able to get Priscilla's operation started in time.

Clara listened solemnly, but she seemed to pick up on the forced carefulness that Eliza tried to exude, and soon she started talking about her day at school. How much fun she had, and how she didn't have to tell people that she only had one leg. Then no one really guessed that one of her legs was fake. She laughed a little and figured that eventually people would figure it out, but she was happy to spend the day feeling normal.

Eliza realized she'd never even told Clara about her own legs.

She laughed a little at Clara thinking she was perfectly normal, when she really wasn't.

But today wasn't the day to show her.

The house felt empty without Hines in it as they walked in, and Clara changed out of her school clothes.

They had a little snack and then went out to feed the animals.

Billy was still there, so they gave him some treats.

She was reading Clara a bedtime story when Hines finally called.

"They got us a spot on a commercial flight. There is a tech going along with us and an ambulance meeting us at the airport tarmac. We'll be whisked away to the hospital in Houston, and she should be in surgery before daybreak."

"That's great news. How is she doing?"

"Same. Her breathing isn't quite as fast, and they brought her temperature down, but she's not awake."

"Okay." Eliza let out a breath. "That makes things easier for you anyway."

"It does. I was able to get my stuff from Miller, but I don't know what's going to be happening, so my updates might be sporadic."

"Thanks. I promise that I won't worry if I don't hear from you. Just... Let us know when you can, okay?"

"I will. Am I on speaker?" he asked.

"You are."

"Great. Clara?"

"Uncle Hines?"

"You'll pray for us?"

"Yes."

"All right, thank you, honey. We can use it."

He said a short prayer, and Eliza closed her eyes, listening to his voice, competent and calm, thinking about how brave he was to be doing all of this for the baby, when he wouldn't do it for himself.

Shortly after the end of his prayer, they hung up, and Eliza tucked Clara in. Then, she realized she hadn't even stopped at Aunt April's house and grabbed her stuff.

She laughed a little, thinking about what a day it had been. But she was able to find some of Hines's sweatpants, roll them up a little, and then a T-shirt that was way too big but made her smile after she took a shower.

It was comforting to lie in his bed, to smell the familiar scent of the man she married, and to fall asleep praying for the life of their baby.

# Chapter 25

*Nine days later...*

L ight shone across the yard as Clara and Eliza sat at the table.
"They're here!" Clara said, jumping up and running to the door.

Hines was able to call them at six o'clock the evening of Priscilla's surgery and let them know that the doctors considered it a success. But she would be in the hospital for a while, although, barring any complications, it should be the last surgery she needed.

They had been in constant contact since then, with Hines giving daily updates, and Clara finding out about her sister before and after school.

Clara and Eliza had known Priscilla and Hines were coming home this evening, but Miller had brought them, since they didn't want to pull Clara out of school where she had adjusted as well as they could expect her to.

"I hope they don't hit Billy!" Clara said as she shrugged her arms into her jacket and threw her shoes on.

"Me, either." Eliza figured Billy would be moving on anytime. He had well and truly matched them up.

She could definitely add herself onto Billy's long list of successful matches.

Although it had been nine days since she had seen the man she married, and she was a little nervous.

Not nervous with the idea that he had changed his mind or anything, just nervous... Because she wanted to see him so bad, she supposed.

She followed Clara out the door and was able to wave to Miller as he pulled back out the drive.

"He could come in. We're eating supper."

"He wants to get home. There's some work to do on the ranch, and he wanted to see if he could lend a hand this evening so everyone there could get to bed a little earlier."

"It was so nice of him to go pick you up," Eliza said, walking toward him as he got the car carrier out of the back seat.

Priscilla, looking chubby and healthy like a normal baby, cooed and kicked her feet.

It made Eliza smile.

"You're beautiful when you smile," Hines said before he reached out a hand and caught Clara as she threw herself into his arms.

"You brought my sister home!" she screamed, holding onto his neck and kissing his cheek.

Eliza thought her exuberant affection made Hines's eyes water, but she couldn't be sure.

He set Clara down and held out an arm for Eliza.

Eliza glided into it slightly slower than Clara had.

"I missed you," she whispered as he lowered his head.

"I missed you too. It's good to be home. And it's even better to see you smiling and out here to meet me."

She grinned, and he kissed her, just a short kiss, but one with a lot of promises. At least, she hoped they were promises, because she was anticipating all the things that could happen after they put the children to bed. But first, she wanted to hold Priscilla and see for herself that she was truly all better.

Reaching into the car, she grabbed the small suitcase and Priscilla's baby bag, then shut the door, and they walked in the house together.

They spent a lot of time talking and listening to Hines tell them how wonderful the doctors were, and what a great baby Priscilla was, and how successful the surgery had been.

Clara held her sister on her lap, snuggling down with her, her cheek resting on Priscilla's forehead.

Priscilla seemed to be just as enraptured to be back with her sister, and she sat on Clara's lap, trying to eat the hair that occasionally fell into her face.

It made them all laugh.

They finished their supper together and did the dishes the same way. Everyone took turns holding Priscilla, with Eliza remarking, "She's going to be so spoiled. She's going to think that she needs to be held all the time, because no one can stand to let her down."

"I know you're right, but I'm finding it hard to care. I'm just so happy to have everyone underneath one roof."

She knew he hadn't been able to go see his sister's grave, which had made her a little sad, but it had been too far from Houston, and he hadn't wanted to leave the hospital for the hours the drive would require. Then, once Priscilla had been discharged, he got the soonest flight out of there. And home.

Together they put the children to bed, lingering over each of them, amazed at how quickly and easily it was to fall in love with the little girls who had moved into their lives.

"We'll be up early for school tomorrow," Eliza said as she reached for Clara's light.

Clara, snuggled down under her covers, smiled, and said, "Bet I beat you up. I like to see the sunrise."

"You just go ahead and try." Eliza grinned, then she turned the light out and said, "I love you. Good night."

"I love you too."

She walked out, smiling at Hines as he closed the door behind them.

He clasped her hand as they walked back down the hall to the living room.

"It's been a long day, and I'm tired, but I wanted to make sure everything really is okay with you," Hines said, threading his fingers through hers and pulling her toward him, until she stood pressed against him, looking up into his dark eyes.

"Everything's fine. Now that you're home. Not that we had a hard time while you were gone, we just... It felt empty here without you."

"The exact same way it would feel if you weren't here," he said.

"Is Priscilla really all better?" she asked, hardly daring to believe it.

"She has to go back for a six-week checkup, then, if that's good, she'll need yearly follow-ups. That's it. Truly." His hold tightened on her. "They're going to move everything to Rockerton, so it won't be quite so much of a trip to have her seen, but I think the doctors there are going to miss her."

"I'm sure they are."

"But I would rather do it that way, because I don't want to be separated from you again. I...spent a lot of time regretting the fact that we got married, and I left immediately."

"I didn't regret that. It made me happy. I have to admit, I looked forward to you coming home."

"Really?" he asked, tilting his head and leaning down just a little as he pressed his lips against her forehead.

"Really. I've been sleeping in your bed. I hope that's okay."

"I hoped you would, but I guess I never said."

"No. But... You're sleeping there with me tonight?"

"If that's okay?"

"Most definitely."

"I realized when I left that I never said this, and I didn't want to tell you for the first time over the phone. I love you. I appreciate the way you stood by me, the way you adjusted to whatever needed to be adjusted to and never questioned the course that you set for yourself. I admire you, I think you're amazing, and you're beautiful too."

"I don't have those pretty words, but I can say I love you too. And I definitely admire you for traveling the whole way to Houston, especially when we both know that you would prefer to have stayed here. It warms my heart that you would do that for someone that you love. And I knew that if you would do it for Priscilla, you would do it for me. And that made me love you even more."

They smiled at each other, and Eliza was grateful that they had the opportunity to talk to each other about that. Like him, she hadn't wanted to say it over the phone, but she'd been tempted to, just because of the lesson of Connie, where she never knew when she was going to lose someone, and she didn't want to have any regrets.

"I'm grateful for the life I have. I love it. And I want to make every day the best it can be," Hines whispered next to her ear before he trailed his lips across her cheek.

"Every day with you," she whispered softly before he kissed her.

Enjoy this preview of *Just a Cowboy's Love Song*, just for you!

# Just a Cowboy's Love Song

## Chapter 1

J ones hurried down the street, casting a quick glance behind him.

Thankfully he'd left his niece, Florence, at home in the duplex they'd just rented in Sweet Water, North Dakota.

Because the cow was gaining on him.

His horns, at least two feet long on each side of his head, were enough to scare anyone, even someone who worked out regularly as he did.

He didn't quite break into a run, but he lengthened his stride. He didn't particularly want to be seen running from a cow.

He managed to take another ten strides or so before he shot another glance over his shoulder.

Somehow, even though the cow didn't look like it was working hard at all, it had managed to gain on him.

He could almost feel the hot breath on the backs of his arms.

Sweat broke out on his brow, and his heart pounded like he'd been jogging for six miles instead of walking for two blocks.

He tucked the takeout that he'd gotten from the diner in town up under his arm.

He had no groceries in the house, and the takeout was all he had to feed his niece. He really didn't think this cow wanted the takeout; he was leaning more toward the idea that the cow wanted *him*.

Still, he hoped both the takeout and himself would manage to make it to the duplex before the cow. What did cows do?

Did they eat people?

Or was he just going to grind him into a messy pulp with his horns?

He'd seen enough bull riding to know horns were dangerous.

Speaking of, something brushed the back of his arm, and he would have forgotten his good intentions and broken into a dead sprint, since his house was only two blocks away, except he noticed a young girl walking toward him.

She didn't seem the slightest bit afraid of this cow in front of her and was actually looking at Jones like there might be something wrong with *him*.

She didn't stop, didn't turn, and... Was she talking to the cow?

"Billy? What are you doing following someone down the sidewalk? You have no manners."

The girl was tall, but she looked to be about the same age as Florence, his niece.

He took a deep breath, and maybe he should have stopped, or maybe he shouldn't have tried to keep one eye on the girl and one eye on the cow.

Whatever it was, he didn't see the crack in the sidewalk and tripped over it.

He went down, dropping the takeout and landing on top of it. A jolt of pain went up through his hip, and his elbow scraped on the cement.

It was embarrassing. He was known as being quite athletic. Despite the fact that he was a musician by trade, he hit the gym regularly and looked like it.

It was a blow to his pride to be looking up at the girl from his inglorious position on the sidewalk.

But fear was more like a dagger to his heart as the cow stopped, standing directly over top of him, his horns looking even bigger from that angle.

"Are you okay?" the girl said, coming over and putting one hand on the cow's forehead, pushing.

The cow, acting all docile now that the girl was a witness to their interactions, backed up so that he was able to lower his head and put his nose directly in front of Jones's nose.

He wasn't sure whether that was an improvement or not. Particularly if this cow was hungry and intended to eat him.

He supposed he would rather the beast start at his head. It would make his demise faster and less painful.

"Billy. Stop being a brat. Back up and let the man up." The girl, her tone soft, still sounded irritated. "This is no way to welcome people to town. You're going to scare them away instead of keeping them around."

"Thanks," he said as the cow backed up even farther, making Jones feel like he could get up, even though he scooted backward a little bit before he did so he didn't have to turn his back on the beast.

"Billy is not usually like this," the girl said, shaking her head.

He wanted to say, "What? Does he typically eat people feetfirst?" But he didn't.

"He doesn't usually chase people down?" he said instead.

"Nah. He loves to be petted, but he doesn't usually target people on the sidewalk."

Jones looked down at his ruined takeout. He had been hoping to be able to get back to his duplex and take it easy for the rest of the day. He supposed that idea was out of the question.

But he didn't want to go back to the diner either. If this cow was attacking innocent people on the sidewalk, he might need to find a different town to settle down in for a while.

"I'm sorry about your food," the girl said, looking at the smashed white Styrofoam boxes on the ground.

He shook his head, bending over and shaking the food out of the boxes before picking the containers up. "It's not your fault. It's mine. I didn't see the crack in the sidewalk."

"I distracted you," the girl said.

He shook his head. It wasn't her fault.

"I'm Jones," he said, putting both boxes in one hand and holding his other out for the girl to shake.

She smiled a little, the way he would imagine Florence would if some strange man offered to shake her hand. Like it made her feel like she was a grown-up. Then she took his hand and shook it with a grip that was surprisingly firm. "I'm Toni."

"Nice to meet you, Toni."

"It's nice to meet you too. I... I guess you're new in town?"

"Is it that obvious?"

"Well, not really, except everyone in town knows Billy. That's the steer."

Not a cow. A steer. He tried to take note of the difference.

"Oh. I guess that was an introduction." He eyed the steer. "I would say it's nice to meet him, but I haven't determined that as of yet."

The girl giggled, and Jones smiled despite himself.

He wasn't really angry at the animal. Getting angry at a cow seemed silly, but he had to say he was annoyed. He wasn't used to being chased down the sidewalk and forced to feel like he needed to run for his life.

The ruined food magnified that feeling.

The girl looked at the sidewalk, and then she lifted her head quickly as though she just thought of something. "My mom has food in the crockpot for tonight. It's really good. And... I know she's going to be working because she said she had a late meeting, but I know she wouldn't mind if you came over and ate some?"

"Oh, I couldn't invite myself like that," Jones said. "Plus, my niece...lives with me." He stumbled over that because he still hadn't gotten used to explaining that his niece was now his. It wasn't that long ago that his sister died in the airplane crash.

"I promise you, Mom always makes a lot, and then we eat the leftovers. But people are always welcome at our table. Mom says that all the time."

Jones shook his head and moved a little. The girl moved with him, and they ended up walking side by side toward his house.

He didn't look back, but he had the feeling the cow, *steer*, was still following him.

He managed not to run.

"I couldn't impose like that."

The girl lifted a shoulder like it didn't matter. "If you change your mind, we live right up here."

"Interesting. I live up here too. I just rented half of the duplex right there."

"You're our new neighbor!" Toni said, her jaw dropping as she looked at him with wide eyes. "I saw there was someone moving in before I left for school today, but I didn't see you. I thought there might be a girl my age."

"I think Florence probably is your age."

"Then you have to come for supper! Whatever time you want. Like I said, Mom will be working so it'll just be me, and I'll wait until you guys show up."

Jones had already declined two or three times, and so he didn't shake his head again. It wouldn't hurt to go over to the neighbors' house and have supper.

Maybe, once the ranch remodel was finished, which shouldn't be long now that he was here to oversee the work, he could invite her and her mom out to eat there, and maybe they'd have animals by then and they'd enjoy looking around the ranch.

He wasn't sure what all the ranch was going to have eventually. His sister had been the one with all the big plans. He'd inherited that along with half of everything she left. The other half went to Florence, and he managed it until she turned eighteen.

The thought of his sister and her plane accident still sent a sharp knife of pain down his ribs, and he pulled his mind away.

It might have been a year, but it hardly felt that long.

Although he was able to think of it now without the sad longing and the deep desire to somehow bring her back that he used to have.

"We have a little table on our porch. You'll see when we get there. I'll just bring everything out and set it on that. If you want to come out and eat with me, you can. And if you don't, don't feel like you have to. The weather is nice enough that I'll be happy eating outside, so you'll be doing me a favor."

Jones looked down at the girl. He knew, in the year since his sister had died, that Florence was lonely. She'd often mentioned that she'd like to have a little brother or sister.

Maybe this girl was lonely too.

"All right. I'll watch for you to go out on your porch, and I'll come over."

He should get out and meet the neighbors anyway. This would be a good way to do that. Even if he didn't meet the mom. Or the dad. Although she hadn't mentioned a dad.

He didn't ask though; that could be a sensitive subject. After all, if someone asked Florence where her parents were for the first six months after her mother's death, she would have started to cry.

Now, he thought that she was slowly healing as he was. And he didn't think she would break down. But...it would definitely make her sad.

So, he looked around for something neutral to talk about, and out of the corner of his eye, he saw the steer was still following them.

"Who owns that steer anyway?" he asked, refraining from saying that they needed to get their animal and make sure he was penned up.

"The town. No one really knows who exactly owns him, and we all kind of take care of him. He's like our own town mascot. We even use him in the petting zoo when we have a festival in town. The kids love him."

"I see." Well, there went that idea. Apparently he was going to be dealing with the steer every time he set foot out of his house since he seemed to be a cow magnet.

"Does he normally chase people down and eat them?" he asked, trying to put a teasing tone in his voice but not entirely sure he succeeded.

"No. You're the first." Toni must have caught the teasing note, because her eyes twinkled when she looked up at him.

He smiled down at her and thought again that she would make a perfect playmate for Florence. Maybe it was a good thing he had accepted her dinner invitation.

He was pretty sure Florence wouldn't turn it down either, and she would possibly have someone to hang out with on her first day of school. There were only a couple of weeks left before summer break, but he was going to enroll her anyway. She had such upheaval in her young life so far, he wanted to give her a sense of normalcy if he could.

They reached the steps of the duplex, his side on the right, Toni's on the left. He saw the table she meant. Some kind of privacy shield hung above the railing that separated the two sides.

He didn't think his new neighbors were going to be annoying, but if they were, that privacy shield would probably come in handy.

"It will be about thirty minutes until I have the food ready, but you can come out whenever you want to."

"Thanks." They separated, and he walked into his house, humming under his breath.

That was new. Since his sister's death, the idea of singing had been depressing. He definitely didn't hum out of happiness. Except, now he was. Interesting.

You can continue reading by getting *Just a Cowboy's Love Song* .

# A Gift from Jessie

*View this code through your smart phone camera to be taken to a page where you can download a FREE ebook when you sign up to get updates from Jessie Gussman! Find out why people say, "Jessie's is the only newsletter I open and read" and "You make my day brighter. Love, love, love reading your newsletters. I don't know where you find time to write books. You are so busy living life. A true blessing." and "I know from now on that I can't be drinking my morning coffee while reading your newsletter – I laughed so hard I sprayed it out all over the table!"*

*Claim your free book from Jessie!*

# Escape to more faith-filled romance series by Jessie Gussman!

***The Complete Sweet Water, North Dakota Reading Order:***
Series One: Sweet Water Ranch Western Cowboy Romance (11 book series)
Series Two: Coming Home to North Dakota (12 book series)
Series Three: Flyboys of Sweet Briar Ranch in North Dakota (13 book series)
Series Four: Sweet View Ranch Western Cowboy Romance (10 book series)

***Spinoffs and More! Additional Series You'll Love:***
Jessie's First Series: Sweet Haven Farm (4 book series)
Small-Town Romance: The Baxter Boys (5 book series)
Bad-Boy Sweet Romance: Richmond Rebels Sweet Romance (3 book series)
Sweet Water Spinoff: Cowboy Crossing (9 book series)
Holiday Romance: Cowboy Mountain Christmas (6 book series)
Small Town Romantic Comedy: Good Grief, Idaho (5 book series)
True Stories from Jessie's Farm: Stories from Jessie Gussman's Newsletter (3 book series)
Reader-Favorite! Sweet Beach Romance: Blueberry Beach (8 book series)
Cowboy Mountain Christmas Spinoff: A Heartland Cowboy Christmas (9 book series)
Blueberry Beach Spinoff: Strawberry Sands (10 book series)

Printed in the USA
CPSIA information can be obtained
at www.ICGtesting.com
LVHW011716240724
786348LV00016B/937

9 781953 066831